Crystal lost all sense of time or place. Clasped in Brett's arms, she felt a new sensuous world had been created. A place lovelier than earth, with colors sparking from the heat, burning with more brilliance than the brightest star.

"Oh, God, Crystal," Brett murmured, ending the kiss by speaking huskily against her lips. "You'll have to give them up," he moaned, raking his hands over her faded denims, revealing his desire.

"Huh?" she mumbled, insensible to anything other than the loud beating in her chest, as heated blood coursed through burning flesh.

"Your lovers," he muttered, planting biting kisses between the words. "Get rid of them. I'm all you need."

ABOUT THE AUTHOR

Jo Ann Algermissen taught school for seventeen years before turning to writing romances. She and her husband and their two children live in Texas, where Jo Ann is learning to ride horses—and has the bruises to prove it. You can find out work by this talented author under the pseudonym Anna Hudson.

Capture the Sun

JO ANN ALGERMISSEN

Harlequin Books

TORONTO • NEW YORK • LONDON
AMSTERDAM • PARIS • SYDNEY • HAMBURG
STOCKHOLM • ATHENS • TOKYO • MILAN

Published July 1984

First printing May 1984

ISBN 0-373-16064-X

Chapter One

"It's what American women want to see," Mike Kaplan, editor of *St. Louis City* magazine, said.

"Another winner of the Pulitzer prize," Crystal observed with a wry smile.

Avoiding her eyes, Mike replied gruffly, "Somebody has to do it, and I can hardly give this assignment to Chad."

Crystal Lake's smile became a chuckle as she visualized the expression on Chad's face had he been given this less-than-illustrious assignment.

"Okay, boss," she agreed, which was all she could do. "If it's what snaps the heartstrings of American women, I'll give it to them in glorious color."

"No models," he instructed. "Strictly what's on the street, at the sports field, in the parks."

Crystal's mobile face scowled. "Do I need releases?"

"In triplicate. No lawsuits." The middle-aged, gray-headed editor's hands began riffling through the stack of surveys from a previous *SLC* edition. "E.B.S. . . . you'll get ideas from the comments on these. Take them with you." A sheaf of papers a foot deep was thrust toward her. "Some of them should have been written on asbestos; the edges are charred. Be selective."

"Ah, yes," Crystal teased, "don't besmirch the staid reputation of the *St. Louis City* magazine." She lowered her voice to a gravelly pitch, imitating her boss. "Stretch the imagination of the reader. Border the lines of convention, but never cross into vulgarity."

"Save the imitations for Rich Little, unless you're considering changing jobs," Mike threatened lightheartedly, unable to stop his lips from slanting upward.

Tucking the bundle of surveys in the crook of her arm as a mother would a small child, Crystal rose to her feet. Noting his repressed smile, she flicked an imaginary cigar, eyebrows wriggling up and down Groucho Marx style, and said before exiting, "Say the right words and the magic birdie will appear. . . ."

"Eyes. Buns. Shoulders . . . as assigned." He

paused. The attempt to stifle the smile was no longer necessary, as he delivered his words in a no-nonsense voice. "And, Crystal, stay off the day-care story. You're making waves."

Silently congratulating herself for not stumbling at the mention of her secret pet project, Crystal waved her fingers limply and scooted out the door backward. Crossing the copy room, heading for the office she shared with Chad Brewster, she contemplated his reaction to her new assignment. Automatically her shoulders straightened into military stiffness.

The lines had been delineated the day she was hired. Chad did the solid investigative reporting; Crystal was delegated the fluff assignments. Women were hired in the previously all-male field, but they were still on the flip side of the society page. The weight of the surveys she carried would be the heaviest part of this work.

Plunking her load down, she grimaced at the broad, knowing smile on Chad's face.

"I volunteer," he said, flipping a standard release form onto the stack.

The undecipherable scrawl on the bottom line of the paper reflected the unkempt nature of its owner. Slight of build, medium in height, with eyes enlarged by the lenses in his glasses, Chad Brewster lacked two of the three items deemed sexy by the reading public. My dogs have better eyes and shoulders, she mused, smiling at the comparison to her terriers.

Leaning back in the desk chair, Crystal smirked. "Show me your stuff."

"I am," Chad replied, blinking his gray eyes and flexing his skinny arms.

Crystal was prepared for his predictable conceit, but nevertheless found it obnoxious. Why would he set a precedent by reacting in a professional manner? She fought to make a noncommital-type response and failed.

"Stand up, turn around, and drop your drawers," she ordered in a crisp tone.

"I've been waiting to hear those exact words for years. Why am I disappointed when I *do* hear them?" he asked mockingly while remaining seated.

"Probably because you don't want REJECTED stamped on the back of your Fruit of the Loom," Crystal answered with sticky sweetness.

Dramatically Chad covered his face with both hands. Noisy pretend sobs competed with the scuffing sound his feet were making on the floor. Crystal observed the immature, low-quality comedy performed by the shrewd, competitive, back-stabbing reporter before rolling her honey-colored eyes heavenward and counting the discolored acoustical tiles on the ceiling.

"Wounded. I'm mortally wounded," he sobbed.

"A pin prick in your overly inflated ego hardly qualifies you for the emergency room."

The pretense ended abruptly as his hands dropped. His dry eyes narrowed into slits. Picking up the release form, he slowly began tearing it in half. "You're missing the opportunity of a lifetime."

"Tryouts for the boys' choir are on Wednesday. If you make it, I'll be certain your picture is front and center." The broad grin she gave him took the sting from the words. After all, like it or not, she did share an office with him.

"I'm going to get my jollies watching you ask unsuspecting males to sign these," he jeered, waving the two halves in front of her face. "The majority of the male population rejects the idea of E.B.S., or of women rating men on a scale of one to ten."

"Why?" she countered. "Men coined the phrase 'perfect ten.' Let them reap the consequences: eyes, buns, and shoulders."

"Most men think women should be kept *behind* the stove, *over* the washing machine, and *in* the bed."

"Mmmm. . . ." Crystal was losing interest in

the conversation quickly. She usually did when Chad started his male chauvinist routine. "I always thought being a *kept* woman had other connotations." Dark eyebrow arching upward, Crystal pointed one finger, cocked her thumb, and fired an imaginary pistol. "Roll over and play dead, Rover. I have work to do."

"Just one quick question." A finger punched his slipping spectacles back on the bridge of his nose. "Underneath the tailored pants suit is there a passionate heart? Or is the rumor going around the office true?"

"Which rumor this time? The one about my being a closet nymphomaniac, or a frigid robot?" Rumors were rampant due to her reticence. Others babbled about their love life in vivid detail. Crystal didn't; thus rumors and speculation followed her everywhere.

"The one regarding your blood tests," Chad replied smugly, preparing to give the knockout punch in their verbal sparring. "Photography chemicals and printers' ink showed up."

"Guilty as accused, and proud of it," she confirmed, grinning.

Disregarding her office mate's attempt at a verbal putdown, Crystal perused the survey on top of the stack. She couldn't let his barbed tongue distract her from her assignment. Chad lacked subtlety. He wasn't interested in the results of her blood test any more than he was interested in her as a woman. He wanted one thing and one thing only: her resignation.

A rounded, perfectly formed feminine script drew her attention completely away from Chad. "Show me a set of luminous eyes, broad muscular shoulders, and oh-so-firm buns.... Off the television or movie screen, do they exist?"

The words were a challenge. Was Mr. Perfect Body roaming the streets of St. Louis waiting to be photographed? Too bad I can't use male models, she thought silently. The assignment could be completed in record time by simply placing a call through to an agency.

Nothing the public demanded was easy. The worst part was their fickleness. By the time the article hit the streets, women would find the perfectly rounded *navel* at the top of their sex list.

Browsing several pages at a time through the pile, Crystal tried to find good points in the assignment. Fluff could be fun if she approached it with a sense of humor. She could imagine the look on a macho male face as the shutter clicked ... focused not on the toothpaste smile, but on the cut of his pants.

The technique she had used on previous assignments to get signatures on release forms should work. It was simple and effective. Flatter and flirt while taking pictures, and then demurely ask for the signature. The task would be completed with finesse, something Chad was sadly lacking. Being a woman had advantages, and Crystal used them guiltlessly.

After reading several in the asbestos category, she mentally scoffed at the idea of the male physique being all important. Experience had taught her beauty on the inside was more important than the packaging. Too often beautiful people relied on their appearance rather than developing their personality or potential.

"Sour grapes?" she mouthed silently, analyzing her own attributes. Late bloomer, she answered. Crystal remembered being a tall, lanky, gawky child with a mouthful of metal throughout her teenage years.

The most humiliating description, which capsulized her lack of beauty, was a conversation she had eavesdropped on during a sleepover her older brother, Gus, was having a month before the junior-senior prom.

"Good personality," the boy next door had said disparagingly.

"Too brainy for me," the deeper voice of the high school star quarterback stated, "but a great tennis partner."

"Come on, guys," Gus had coaxed, "*someone* has to take her!"

Mortified by the frank discussion, her ear,

which was pressed to the wall between their rooms, sizzled. She recalled having childishly plotted revenge. The toilet seat was vaselined. Aftershave was dumped and refilled with sweet, cloying perfume. New razor blades were thrown out and replaced with ones severely nicked. Bristles from an old brush were sliced off the handle and thrown into their sleeping bags. The best part had been listening to them moan and groan and blame each other for the pranks.

Smiling at the memory, Crystal's eyes flicked over two more surveys. Revenge did not erase the hurt; time and nature had. The gleam of stainless steel had been removed, leaving a wide, sparkling smile. High, prominent cheekbones and widely spaced honey-colored eyes welcomed being cosmetically accented. Her dark hair, when unplaited, was full, shiny, and waist-long.

The memory vaporized when Crystal spotted an entire form covered with large capital letters: EYES! Dark, pale, smoky, clear, haunted, merry, angry, tender...EYES!

Picking her camera out of the case, Crystal unloaded the completed roll of film and replaced it with fresh film. She snapped shut the cover and grinned in anticipation. These pictures would not change the course of world politics, but it would be interesting to discover, purely in a scientific manner, what physically was most attractive to the photographer.

"I'm off," she said, more to herself than to Chad.

Several rolls of film later, Crystal ordered a sandwich at a local delicatessen for a late lunch. Satisfied with the variety of eyes she had managed to photograph, she crossed the busy street and perched herself on the steps in front of the Robert E. Lee monument. The small pocket park was a green haven in the busy metropolis. Eating lunch in the shade of the granite statue was as effective as replacing a dead battery in her strobe.

Her morning's work foremost in her thoughts, she speculated about the unseeing granite eyes overhead. What could Lee's eyes have revealed? Had they narrowed speculatively when Lincoln had asked him to head the Union forces? As his horse plodded back to Richmond, had doubts shrouded his decision not to turn his back on Virginia? A graduate of West Point, his eyes must have narrowed as they scoured over battle plans. Had the eyes reflected the despair of defeat when he surrendered his forces to Grant at the Appomattox Court House? Was there relief expressed when the opposing general, who later became president, allowed almost thirty thousand Confederates to keep their horses for the long trek home? Crystal shook her head in sorrow for the Confederate leader. He had died a man without a country.

Had Matthew Brady, famed photographer of the War Between the States, focused his camera on the eyes of the generals, their own personal stories could have been revealed. An assignment of that nature would be more to my liking, Crystal mused, still munching on the ham and cheese sandwich. Brought back to the twentieth century, her photographer's eyes scanned the occupants of the park benches.

Inwardly she smiled at the portraits of contrast on the green, wooden slats of the benches. A mother, proudly watching her child play, was seated near a meticulously dressed career woman whose face was tipped back, absorbing the sun. Two uniformed deliverymen were on the same bench as a scruffy looking teenager. The park benches seldom displayed segregation according to wealth, occupation, or age.

In the corner of her peripheral vision, she saw two women dressed in similar office attire chatting affably while covertly glancing at a businessman seated on the opposite end of the same bench. Crystal could tell they were attracted to the man. Why?

Analytically she dissected his appearance in a detached manner. Even sitting, she knew he was tall by the length of leg stretched before him. His ankles were casually crossed. Wing-tipped shoes? Must be an executive climbing the corporate ladder, she speculated. Shoes were usually a dead giveaway. The torso of his body was hidden from her view by a copy of *The Wall Street Journal.* Another dead give-away. Studying his face, she could see only the broad brow, straight nose, and lips from a slanted angle. A gentle breeze dislodged the dark, straight hair, blowing it over his forehead. Absorbed in reading the news, he didn't appear to notice.

Raise your head, she commanded telepathi-cally. *I want to see your eyes.* Slowly, as though receiving the silent message, his head lifted. They were dark. Darker than midnight, but capturing the rays of the sun, they shone brightly. As his lips tilted upward, tiny lines fanned at the corners of each eye, completing the smile. He had the most expressively beauti-ful eyes she had seen all day.

Automatically she removed the lens cap and swung the camera in front of her face. Zooming in, she caught the rounding of his eyes as they showed surprise, then again the smiling eyes. Her right index finger pressed repeatedly. Unaware of even moving, she shortened the distance between them.

"Why don't you take a picture or two, lady? It'll last longer." The snide question was asked by the female office worker sitting nearby.

Camera in place, Crystal swiveled slightly, aiming at the two women. "I'm a professional photographer. Would you mind my taking your picture also?"

Both women preened, readily agreeing. "Newspaper?"

"*St. Louis City* magazine. I'm doing an article on male sex appeal." Moving a few feet away, she tried to focus the picture to encompass the man and the two women. All she saw through the viewfinder was two women and a newspaper with legs.

"Would you mind lowering the paper?" she requested softly.

"Yes. I would." Three words delivered scarcely a pitch above a growl came from behind the black-and-white print.

"Surely you don't object to being admired by two attractive women, do you?" she coaxed. The women twittered at the compliment. "You have extremely sexy eyes," Crystal said, flattering him further. "Don't be embarrassed. Put the paper down and let me take a few more shots."

"No, thanks," the stranger replied, keeping the barrier firmly in place and snapping it for negative emphasis.

Crystal chuckled. "You're not on the Ten Most Wanted List at the post office, are you?"

"No. And I don't want to be on the Ten Most Wanted List for lusty females who read your magazine, either."

"Press shy?"

"Most definitely," he agreed.

"Could I persuade you to sign releases for the pictures I've already taken?"

"No!"

"Come on, mister," one of the secretaries pleaded. "I'd love to have a picture of the three of us. Or just the two of us, if you prefer." Her mascara-coated eyelashes fluttered enticingly.

"Thanks a lot!" her friend said sarcastically, disliking the prospect of being left out.

"Would your husband . . . boyfriend . . . boss, whatever, enjoy seeing our picture plastered in a glossy scandal rag?"

"Scandal rag?" Crystal was aghast at the slur. "Now just a minute . . ." she said, beginning to refute his claim.

"Thanks, anyway, sweetie," the secretaries said in unison, gathering up their brown lunch bags and purses.

The woman who had originally tried to coax

the recalcitrant man added, "My Ralph would have a fit if he suspected I was picking up men on my lunch hour."

Before Crystal could change their minds, they had quickly departed.

"Thanks, mister," she said dryly. "You cost me a great picture."

"You're welcome," she heard from behind the elevated paper.

Was that laughter she heard in his voice? Surely not.

"Would you reconsider signing the release form? I'd really appreciate it."

"No, but thanks for the compliment."

"You're welcome," she said sweetly, still harboring thoughts of convincing him to change his mind. He really did have the most spectacular eyes. Mentally she clicked the dark eyes into a famous face . . . Omar Sharif.

Unclasping the twist latch on her camera case, she extracted a release form and attached a business card. "If you have a change of heart, call me."

As *The Wall Street Journal* folded forward, she felt the intensity of the dark chocolate eyes as they swept over her. They did not strip away the clothing but gently traced the contours of her body. An expressive dark eyebrow lifted slightly at the tip.

"May I call you without changing my mind?"

The muscles in the calves of her legs contracted as her toes curled. The husky quality in the southern drawl was as sexy as the gleam sparking from his eyes. Don't call; ask now, was her first impulse. Jiminy Cricket, she chastized, sexy eyes and a seductive voice hardly serve as a formal introduction. She didn't even know his name!

"Brett Masterson," he said, introducing himself as he read her business card. "Crystal Lake? Nice pen name," he commented.

"I'll tell my mother you like it," she rejoined, wishing for the umpteenth time her parents had chosen normal names for their offspring.

"Not a pen name?" he acknowledged, rising to his feet and offering his hand.

The warmth emanating from his eyes made Crystal hesitantly place her hand in his. Immediately the back of her hand was covered. Rationally she knew she should withdraw from the intimate handclasp, but couldn't. His eyes beckoned her to investigate the hidden source of light, to sway forward instead of retreating.

"There should be a law requiring you to wear sunglasses," she murmured, not realizing she had spoken out loud.

"The same law would require you to cover the sprinkling of freckles across your nose," he whispered, smiling broadly.

Self-consciously she withdrew her hand and brushed it over the freckles she had never outgrown.

"My dad used to say a woman without freckles was like a moonlit night without stars. They are more enticing than a beauty mark," he complimented, his voice remaining hushed.

Crystal was caught suspended somewhere between the silver sparkling in his eyes and the golden words sliding from his sensuous lips. The sensation of being swept up and carried high above the people around them made her skin tingle.

Mesmerized, she started, then gasped audibly when she felt her knees being grasped and tightly held. Relief flooded through her when she saw small hands, rather than long, tapered fingers, grabbing and clutching the navy blue fabric of her trousers.

"My mommie is lost," the small intruder said, latching on tighter. "Can you find her?"

Leaning down, Crystal touched the soft blond curls on the child's head and asked in a soothing voice, "Where was she before you lost her?"

China-blue eyes raised, and a single tear slid

down one rounded cheek. A grubby finger pointed toward the statue. "Over there."

Dropping to his haunches, Brett said, "Let's go see if we can find her."

"Mmmm-kay," the boy answered, wiping the tear away with his fist and leaving a smudgy trail in its place.

Brett swept the child up and held him in the comforting manner of a father. "What's your name, young man?"

"Timothy O'Shea."

"Well, Timothy O'Shea, let's take a quick look and see if we can come up with one lost mother."

Crystal was already scanning the park. Mrs. O'Shea couldn't be too far away and was probably frantic.

"What does your mommie look like?" Crystal quizzed.

"She's pretty ... like you, but she's fat," he replied with a smile. His small hands made a rounded motion in front of his chubby tummy.

"Tim-o-thy! Tim-o-thy!"

Brett, Crystal, and Timothy all heard the wail at the same time. Squirming, Timothy slipped down the front of Brett, yelling, "Mommie. Mommie."

Small feet dashed toward the pregnant woman stepping from behind a row of tall bushes.

Timothy's arms circled her knees just as they had Crystal's. The mother's arms wrapped around his small shoulders.

"I've looked all over for you, son," she said, gently reprimanding the boy. "Doesn't it scare you to get lost?"

Timothy shook his head negatively. "I wasn't lost. You were." Pointing his finger at the two adults standing nearby, he said, "This pretty lady and her daddy were going to find you."

"Husband, not daddy," the young mother automatically corrected, bracing her hands against her back and easing into an upright position.

"Do you get lost often?" Crystal asked, deciding not to muddle the conversation by explaining the nonexisting relationship between herself and Brett Masterson.

Winking, the mother replied, rubbing her stomach, "Only since Timothy's feet grew faster than the baby."

Timothy, no longer interested in grown-up talk, was patting the side of the camera case. His small fingers inquisitively twisted the brass catch.

"It's a camera," Crystal explained, stooping down to be at eye level with the curious youngster. "Would you let me take your picture?" Crystal's eyes caught the consenting nod of the proud mother.

"Uh-huh!" Clapping his hands together, he jumped up and down enthusiastically. "Will I get to sit on Santa's lap?"

The three adults laughed. "You can tell how often we have pictures taken," Mrs. O'Shea said, wiping the tearstain off Timothy's face.

"No Santa Claus this time, Timothy. These will be special spring pictures." Crystal glanced around, searching for the ideal backdrop. "How about over there by the daffodils and tulips?"

"Shouldn't you tell Mrs. O'Shea about the nature of the article you're doing *before* you take the pictures?" Brett drawled.

"It's an article on the most sexy features of a man," Crystal responded, smiling at Mrs. O'Shea, then scowling over her shoulder toward Brett. "Your son has beautiful eyes."

"You're telling me! An identical set of eyes attracted me to his father."

"You'll have to sign a release form," she managed to say before Brett could inject the information.

"Sure. I wish Bill was here for you to photograph."

"See, Hubby?" Crystal said spiritedly with poorly concealed triumph. "Not all people are camera shy." She cast him a why-don't-you-sign-the-release-sport grin before striding toward the flower bed.

A low chuckle followed her departing footsteps.

"See you later . . . love," Brett called.

Crystal didn't acknowledge the possibility of another encounter or the endearment with anything other than a slight shrug of her shoulders. She had work to do. Work that took less energy and was more profitable than controlling the emotions the stranger had provoked. Temporary insanity, she chided. What hidden element had she seen in his eyes that she had been unable to capture all day in the multitude of pictures she had taken?

Tipping her head up, she quickly decided it was merely the filtered sunlight coming through the branches of the elm trees. Rationally she decided the depth of his dark eyes had captured the sun's rays. Nothing mystical or magical had happened.

Bending to one knee a short distance from Timothy, she checked the light meter. If her theory was correct, Timothy's eyes would have the same quality when photographed. She would use every ounce of professional skill in an effort to get the same quality in the bright blue eyes facing her camera.

"Timothy, can you spot the squirrel jumping from limb to limb over there?"

His blue eyes rounded excitedly.

"I see it," he shouted. "Can we catch it and take it home, Mommie?"

Snap. Crystal caught the wistfulness in his eyes.

"No pets. You know the apartment rules."

Snap. Disappointment made the eyelids droop a fraction.

"Once the baby is born, we'll be moving back to the country. Rex wouldn't like it if you brought home a new pet, would he?"

The shutter clicked, catching the expression of longing. Mrs. O'Shea kneeled down and stretched out her arms with compassion toward her son. "I love you, Timmy," she consoled softly.

Crystal moved behind Mrs. O'Shea and clicked the camera just as Timothy hugged her.

"I love you too, Mommie."

Tilting her head toward the source of light, Crystal marveled at how similar the expression in the blue eyes had been to the dark eyes she had been hypnotized by earlier. Sighing, she congratulated herself on correctly interpreting the situation. It was all a trick in the lighting. Theory proved.

With a squiggle and a wiggle, Timothy disengaged himself and bounded toward Crystal. "Can we take the pictures now?"

Laughing, she answered, "I did. You were super fantastic."

"Will I be famous and get paid a zillion dollars?"

"Would you settle for an ice cream sundae dripping with chocolate instead?" she bargained.

"Yippee! Ice cream is better anyway."

Skipping in the direction of the ice cream parlor at the edge of the park, he chanted while jumping over the cracks in the sidewalk, "Ice cream yummy . . . money yuckie. Ice cream yummy . . ."

"Thank goodness his father isn't around," Mrs. O'Shea commented, grinning. "Bill is a banker."

"A banker? Are you certain you won't have any hassle at home if I use one of Timothy's pictures?" Crystal asked, recalling the words of Brett and Chad.

"Not all bankers are staid. In fact, I'm the one who makes certain Bill's suit, tie, and shirt coordinate. He couldn't care less about the bankers' image."

"Well, if he does object, give me a call."

"Object? He'll probably avidly read the article and quiz me over the contents," she replied, laughing merrily.

Joining her in laughter, Crystal quickened the pace as they neared the busy street.

"Timmy! You wait for us or no ice cream," Mrs. O'Shea called to her son.

Hand in hand, the three of them crossed the intersection. A fattening half an hour later, Crystal bid the mother and son good-bye and flagged down a cab. Normally she would have used public transportation, but she had to make her 4:30 appointment. Mentally she clocked out at *SLC*. On her own time, not company time, she would conduct the interviews and do the necessary research for her private investigative project.

Mike getting wind of her off-hours research was a good sign rather than a bad one. Evidently the interviews she had conducted were causing ripples on the calm waters of one of the corporate lakes. Good, she thought. The glad-hand smiles she had faced must have masked worried grimaces. No wonder they had not allowed her to interview employees. They were sitting on a time bomb threatening to explode, and they knew it.

The warning Mike had given was a mild slap on the wrist. One to recognize, but not be overly concerned about. When the bomb burst, flinging shrapnel all over the place, she would have enough facts and figures to justify the investigation.

She staunchly believed day care was a more

valid company expenditure than a two-martini lunch, a company car for an executive, or extravagant travel expenses. Compiling the hidden details of expense accounts and fringe benefits would confirm her hunch that nipping in the waistline of the executive paunch could provide the necessary funds to operate on-site facilities for the children of working mothers.

As the cab drew to the curb Crystal handed the driver fare plus tip. The dark eyes of the driver nearly made her consider being late. Their size and deep color reminded her of the stranger in the park. Crystal patted her camera, but refrained. There was something missing in his eyes. The spark of fire that changed the dark depths to a warm glow wasn't there.

I'll find it again, she thought. *All I have to do is keep looking and catch the sunlight when it is just right.*

Chapter Two

Several days later, following a lead, Crystal arrived at the telephone company. She had heard from a friend of a friend that Annette Harper was actively pushing for the same goal Crystal was researching. This could be the break she had been waiting for. A woman on the inside ready to tell all.

"Crystal Lake," she said to the receptionist, introducing herself. "I'm here for an appointment with Mrs. Harper."

"Mrs. Harper is expecting you. Go right on in," the smiling receptionist replied, pointing to an inner office door.

Rapping once, she entered the less-than-plush office whose only redeeming feature was a large window allowing sunlight into the otherwise dreary office.

"Miss Lake?" A small, dark-haired woman in her mid-thirties extended her hand toward Crystal in a mechanical way.

Crystal reached over the steel desktop. "Mrs. Harper, thank you for taking time from your business schedule to see me." *Start the interview with a touch, then warmth and sincerity.* "Call me Crystal, please." *Make the interview as informal as possible.*

"*Annette.* What can I do for you?" she asked politely.

"I'm interested in exploring the possibilities of corporate day care in public utilities. What is your viewpoint?"

Annette pushed back deeper into the desk armchair. "Officially, and I assume you prefer an official statement, the telephone company is striving to keep the cost of owning and using a phone minimal for our customers. Rate hikes are unpopular."

"Then, officially, the company's concerns for the welfare of the general public is greater than the welfare of the individuals you employ?" Crystal probed shrewdly.

Fingers locked together, Annette placed them carefully on her desk. "Crystal, the phone company has arranged for a variety of alternative plans."

"Such as?"

The buzzing of the telephone on Annette's desk interrupted the discussion.

"Yes?" Annette visibly straightened. "I'm being interviewed by *St. Louis City* magazine." Annette paused, listening closely to the voice coming through the receiver. "Yes, sir. I'll expect you shortly."

Gleaning no information from the one-sided conversation, Crystal pulled out a small note pad and pen and began leafing through the pages of questions she had asked other personnel directors.

"Sorry about that," Annette apologized. "Mr. Masterson, my boss, is interested in the *why*s of your being here. I invited him to join us. Do you mind?"

"Not at all. He can probably add input." *Or output, if he's the man I met in the park.* Crystal squelched the giggle that threatened to slide from her lips. *He probably thinks I'm here gathering information for the E.B.S. story. He'll hotfoot it over here and get the surprise of his life when he realizes I'm here for more than fluff.*

For some unperceived reason the thought of having Brett see her as a serious reporter was intoxicating. More heady than the nightly dreams she had been having about a tall, dark-eyed man pursuing her relentlessly. They were the same type of fantasies she had had as a teenager. Each morning this week she had awakened with a thought reminiscent of adolescent libidinousness. *Why am I attracted to him when he is not attracted to me? Why do I dream about pulling him into my bed when he doesn't bother to call?* The same frustrating thoughts with the same ego-deflating answer: *Look in the mirror.*

Lowering her voice and leaning forward conspiratorially, Crystal asked, "Would you answer a few unofficial, off-the-record questions?"

Annette nodded, but glanced apprehensively at the doorway.

"Do you have children?" Crystal asked quickly.

"Yes. A boy and a girl who are ten and six, respectively."

"What arrangements do you make for them?"

"I employ a daytime housekeeper."

"Expensive?"

"You bet. Sometimes I question the validity of my . . ." The door opened, immediately clamping the words off in midsentence.

Standing, Annette introduced the impeccably dressed executive entering the office. "Crystal Lake, Brett Masterson, head of the Human Resources Department."

The smile hovering on Brett's lips became a full-fledged grin. "I've met Crystal," he said to Annette, taking advantage of the opportunity to use her first name. "Same article?" he queried, dark eyes glowing with mirth.

Clearing her throat to remove the temporary blockage his appearance caused, she answered coolly, "No, sir." The respectful reply was an effort to establish a business relationship. Foolish, she thought, as he swept it aside by dragging a chair from the corner of the office and placing it at her side.

"What can the telephone company do for you, Crystal?" he asked, totally destroying any flimsy pretence.

As she ducked her head, the quick motion dislodged a tendril of long dark hair from the sleek bun at the nape of her neck. It's length brushed softly against her cheek. The sensation was kisslike. Crystal squeezed her eyes shut momentarily, rejecting the fanciful thought. When she glanced up at Annette, she realized several moments had passed without a reply to his direct question.

"We are discussing the feasibility of on-the-premises day care for the children of employees," she said airily, as though it were a topic on the tip of everyone's tongue.

Brett's dark eyes narrowed and flashed toward Annette. "Did the fates bring you two together, Ms Harper, or a well-placed phone call?"

"Fates," Annette answered succinctly.

"You are representing the phone company, not the Employee Relations Board," he reminded his subordinate, ignoring the inquisitive look on Crystal's face. The velvet softness of his deep drawl thinly covered his rigid, steely voice, which was tempered and hard.

"Yes, sir," Annette answered curtly, thrusting her rounded chin forward aggressively.

Amusement lit Crystal's face. This discussion obviously was not new territory for either of them. She was delighted with the possibility of having a coconspirator.

"Would you object to answering a few questions... Brett?" she asked in a saccharine tone.

The dark, handsome profile turned toward her with nonchalance. "I only permit one interview a week. A femme fatale reporter accosted me in the park a few days ago." A chuckle slipped through the stern facade, making chills run up and down Crystal's spine. "My quota is filled." He gestured toward Annette, who had seated herself. "Continue on with Annette as if I weren't here."

"You're too masculine to be set aside as nonexistent," Annette interjected sardonically.

Amen! Getting Annette to reveal the involvement Brett had alluded to would be impossible with him sitting there, editing every word by virtue of his mere presence. The devastating effect he was having on her own composure was enough to ensure complete failure of the interview.

"Nonsense, Annette. *Professional* women disregard the gender of co-workers. I believe those are *your* words...not mine," he countered, smiling at the furrowed brow and annoyed expression Crystal couldn't conceal.

Flushing, Annette made a small, palms-up gesture of appeal to Crystal, who had also felt the censure in the gentle rebuke.

"You were explaining the programs available for employees' children before Brett arrived. Perhaps we should resume there," Crystal prompted, slanting a hopeful look toward Brett. His dark eyes rejected her appeal and locked in on Annette.

The stock answers Crystal received could have come from a tape recorder, or been read in an in-house news bulletin. Not once did she deviate from company policy.

Having interviewed other corporate personnel executives, Crystal could have written the answers to her questions without listening. A corporation might destroy itself with inner strife, but a solid front was presented to any outsider. A reporter was classified as an outsider. Not an ambivalent outsider, but a snoop. The conservative corporate image was as explicit as the wing-tipped black shoes on their executives' feet. Realizing the futility of inquiring further, Crystal closed her note pad, stood, and offered her hand to Annette.

"I appreciate your time and your help."

The warm handclasp of the two professionals would not reveal to an observer the slight pressure that relayed empathy for Annette's precarious position.

"You are quite welcome, Crystal. I was glad to be of service." Again a squeeze that acknowledged Crystal's understanding. The handclasp ended with a silent promise to help each other when not being observed by higher-ups.

Every interview had ended with the same verbal platitude. She knew of the falsity, and they did too. But maybe Annette was willing to take a risk outside of the office. Corporate robots, she mused, glancing from Annette to Brett. Keep the image shiny, untarnished, and well oiled, she mentally jeered.

"If you'll come into my office, I'll sign any release forms you need," Brett offered. The slight grin curving one corner of his lips upward suggested a double meaning.

Crystal realized he was, under the guise of legal technicalities, tempting her with the possibility of releasing the pictures she had taken for the E.B.S. story. Quickly assessing the pros and cons, she nodded her head in agreement and followed him out the door.

Ensconced in his own private, more luxurious office, Crystal handed the necessary forms across the desk. "I appreciate your agreeing to let us use your photograph," she said pointedly.

Toying with the edge of the paper, Brett reclined comfortably into his deeply padded executive chair. "You're too perceptive not to realize I dangled the carrot to afford myself the opportunity of getting you in here."

"*Dangled the carrot?* Why would you entice a workhorse employed by a slick magazine into your inner sanctum?" she asked, combining the innuendos and his stated opinion with a touch of humor.

Brett merely smiled. The answer was held in the appreciative appraisal in the black eyes sweeping over her face. His gaze lingered on her fingers which were busy trying to tuck the loose ends of her hair back in order.

"Perhaps over dinner we could discuss the

merits of tiny toddlers being on the job site with their ambitious mothers."

"Another carrot? Why don't you try another approach?" Crystal scoffed, taking the form he had repeatedly folded from between his fingers.

Instantly her wrist was grasped and she was tugged forward. Off balance, Crystal automatically shifted her weight forward, bracing her left hand in the center of his desk.

"Release my wrist, Mr. Masterson," she said, barely moving her lips.

"Are carrots preferable to brute force?" The wicked glint in his eyes as they hung on her lips made her balance more precarious.

"What happens when I scream?" she questioned threateningly. His grip loosened marginally.

"Go ahead. But don't be embarrassed by the repercussions," he warned ominously.

Crystal saw the tanned skin covering his jaw become taut. Threatening the wolf in his own lair was the height of stupidity. Realizing she could shout until her lungs fell on the desktop without success, she tried another ploy.

"Please, Brett?" she appealed, twisting her wrist.

"That's better," he replied, watching one of her eyebrows wing upward questioningly.

"Much better than the tough woman reporter threatening a thug," he clarified.

Crystal straightened as he released his hold. Wadding the creased form into a compact ball, she considered bouncing it off the mocking face confronting her.

"Grown women don't throw things, regardless of the temptation," he goaded, egging her on, "or justification."

Gracefully pivoting, Crystal stiffly marched to the door. *Wretched, egotistical, overbearing, uptight* . . . The list ceased when he whispered her name.

"Crystal Lake." Never had anyone spoken her name with such appeal. "You scare the hell out of me."

Turning, knees wobbling from the effect his voice had, she mustered every shred of poise stored in her being and replied, "Scared? Is that why you didn't call?"

"As a matter of fact, it is."

She rolled her eyes upward. "Mr. Masterson, try again. That line went out with Rhett Butler," she riposted with droll humor.

While she delivered her short, cutting speech, Brett had sauntered toward her, both hands buried in his pockets. "The famous line was: 'Frankly, my dear, I don't give a damn.' I do give a damn, which is why I didn't call."

"Somewhere I'm certain there is logic in your statement, but it is vague . . . *very* vague."

"Then let me enlighten you. You are not the type of woman to dally with and drop. You're the take-home-to-Momma, buy-a-ring, and marry type. How did you make it to the ripe old age of what, twenty-five, twenty-six, without a wedding ring?"

"Cautiously! I'm a *career* woman doing the work I'm assigned and working toward a better career with better assignments." Pausing meaningfully, she delivered the clincher. "Neither a gorgeous pair of eyes nor a square executive can alter my goals. Even when the eyes belong to the executive."

"Slap and caress," he commented as her hand twisted the doorknob. "Far more effective than carrots. Next time I'll try your tactics."

His hand covered hers as she rotated the knob. Taking a deep gulp she knew could be heard on the other side of the door, Crystal opened it a crack.

"There won't be a next time," she managed to croak out.

"You're underestimating your adversary," he claimed with calm assurance.

"We hardly know each other well enough to be considered enemies," she protested.

The dark eyes, without benefit of the sun,

shone with a clarity all their own. "I've decided to take the risk. I want to know you better. Care to investigate those possibilities?"

The words were so softly spoken they had the unreal quality of being a figment of her imagination. Normally she would have reacted with disgust to the word *want,* but strangely enough, she didn't feel insulted. Quite the opposite. The whisper was too close to her own thoughts. Investigating the possibilities would be more dangerous than reporting the undercover operation of an international spy ring. She wasn't prepared for the hazards of investigating either of them.

Slipping through the door, she left his question dangling between them. Having the last word in any discussion with a male was a goal she seldom abandoned, but this time the only word her heart wanted to say was yes. It was wiser to flee than speak.

"Damn his eyes!" she muttered, striving to build an anger that wasn't there. She propelled herself through the revolving door in the front of the office building in a huff. Spinning back toward the building, she clenched both fists, raised them over her head, and shook them toward the steel, concrete, and glass.

"They won't reduce your bill."

Crystal spun back around, embarrassed by

her atypical behavior. She saw an old man wearily shaking his head at her frustration.

"The rates are so high I had to take my phone out," he complained. "Worked all my life, and I can't afford the basics." Hopelessness marked his face. Shuffling his feet, his slow gait carried him down the sidewalk muttering to himself.

The unsolicited words made Crystal consider another aspect of the day-care picture. Would other senior citizens do without a telephone if her pet project did influence the men at the top of the corporate structure? The words of the elderly man kept repeating themselves.

Stymied at every turn, she fumed. The whole week had been nothing but a bundle of dead ends. It had started with the job assignment, Brett's refusal to sign the release form, then Annette's restrained answers and her own tongue-tied response to Brett's question; now it was ending up with the comments of the man wearily trudging down the street. At the rate she was going, she would have been better off calling in sick with the measles and spending the week in bed with a good book. If destiny had its way, the last chapter of the book would be missing.

Tossing her head back, she laughed. Crazy weeks could be coped with. For the time being she would forget her problems and enjoy what was left of the few remaining hours of mild spring weather.

"T.G.I.F.," she said heartily. *Thank God it's Friday!*

Chapter Three

Dressed in cutoff jeans, red tank top, white athletic socks, and tennis shoes, Crystal yanked the cord, drawing the front draperies aside with a loud swoosh. Great, she thought, seeing another bright, crisp morning. After her usual Saturday morning tennis match with Mike, there would be time to snap a few pictures of tennis buns before lunch.

Crystal grinned, revising the thought. She'd take pictures of tennis bums' buns.

"What a tongue twister," she said to Scotty and Mac, her Scottish terriers. "Tennis bums' buns. Tennis bums' buns. Tennis buns bums'." Repeating the phrase quickly in rapid succession, she found her early-morning tongue not agile enough. Her smile widened at the failure.

"Out you go, pups," she called, sliding back the patio door. She often conversed with the dogs. Living alone led to two choices: talking to the dogs or talking to herself. She did both.

Buns, she mused, striding toward the courts. There had to be a more dignified term. Derriere? No, too feminine. Butt? Too crude. As she shook her head her long dark ponytail swung over her shoulder. Bottom? Hindquarters? Tush? Rejecting all of the substitute words, she came back to the one word that said it all: *buns*.

Shrugging at her inability to come up with another choice of word, she contemplated the upcoming tennis match. The brisk walk to the condominium tennis courts had stretched and warmed up the leg muscles that would be getting a strenuous workout. For a man on the wrong side of fifty, Mike was as quick on the courts as he was behind the editor's desk. Their win-loss record was about even, much to her chagrin.

Crystal waved as she spotted Mike and his wife, Jane, jogging from their end of the complex toward the courts. Acknowledging the wave, Mike continued toward her, and Jane veered off toward the bike paths for her morning exercise. Jane's trim figure was the envy of many of the condo housewives. With a pang Crystal realized she envied her also, but not for the same reason. She envied the close, loving relationship between Jane and her husband. They were the ideal couple. Perhaps the similarity between her own parents and Mike and Jane had influenced her decision to take the *SLC* offer rather than strike out to test her luck on the East coast.

"Morning, Crystal. Ready for another tromping?" Mike inquired, dropping his racket case on the ground by the tall cyclone fence.

"Here or at the office?" she lightly teased.

"Both," he replied glibly. His eyes did a double take of her less-than-glamorous tennis attire. "Aren't those shorts a little ... short?"

"Uh-uh. You're not going to get a psychological advantage by making me worry about my clothes—or my job—while I'm trying to beat the dickens out of you." Mike was adept at dropping small bombs before a round to give himself an edge.

"Would I do something so underhanded?" he asked mildly, not taking offence.

"As a matter of fact, you would. You are a sly old devil, and you know it."

"Not as sly as you have been," he retorted, walking to the opposite side of the court. "Let's hit a few warm-up balls."

Crystal served, lobbing the ball over the net. With great ease Mike returned the serve, blooping the ball toward her. Back and forth the lime-green ball bounced until Mike deflected it upward and caught it.

"My serve," he stated, not offering to let her have the honors.

"Okay, boss," she acquiesced.

Barely to the left of the center court line he stopped.

"I had an interesting call from the telephone company late yesterday afternoon." The speed of the oncoming ball did not leave her time to react to the statement.

"Alley," she called, meaning more than the inaccuracy of the serve.

Stepping behind the line, Mike prepared to poise for a drive with less speed and more spin. "Brett Masterson."

Crystal blocked the serve with her backhand but not the name. "What did he want?" she asked, feigning innocence, eyes following the ball.

Mike dashed forward, slamming the ball across the net before it bounced. Running to the back of the court, Crystal soundly smacked the ball to a similar position on the opposite side and smiled as it sailed beyond his reach, but remained within the boundary lines.

"Family talk to begin with," he baited.

"Family?"

"Yeah. We're cousins on his mother's side,"

he said, explaining the family relationship but not volunteering any further information. "Your point. Love fifteen."

Her point, hell. Mike was going to eke out the damning information a dribble at a time. More accurately, a point at a time.

Hunched forward, ready to return a power-house drive, Crystal bounced from foot to foot. Using a change of pace typical of his style, Mike hit the ball over the net at less than full force. Seconds after she had returned the volley, Mike had her pounding frantically from one side of the back court to the other while he appeared to be standing perfectly still. The more frazzled she became, the wider the grin on his face spread. Point by point, without even working up a sweat, he was wearing her down and winning.

"My game. Your serve," her opponent said, grinning from ear to ear in triumph.

Figuratively Brett Masterson had won the game. The mere mention of his name had broken her concentration and cost her points.

Hands on hips, chest heaving, she glared over the net. "I'll beat the pants off of you this time," she proclaimed, blocking the image of dark eyes from her mind.

"Then do what? I saw your camera case. You going to take a picture of my rear end?" he joked with ribald humor.

"Good idea. Jane would love seeing your pink little cheeks prominently displayed in glorious color, centerfold style."

"Why take a picture when she has the real thing snuggled up to her every night?" he bragged, shaking the object of their discussion in her direction before swaggering to back court.

Loping to the serving line, she lined herself up. "That's not what Jane says." The words were delivered with the same accuracy as the ball.

Mike didn't move a muscle. "Whaddaya mean?" he demanded as the ball banged into the fence.

"Fifteen love," Crystal called gleefully. Let him stew for a while.

"Dirty tennis," Mike sneered.

"You ought to know," she replied sweetly.

"Jane doesn't discuss our love life," Mike stated, switching the conversation back on course.

"Right," Crystal agreed truthfully.

When she tossed the ball high, slamming her racket in a powerful downward stroke, the ball whizzed over the net. Mike was ready. The game had become a duel. Crystal was no longer the only one pushing her physical limits in order to return the ball.

"Fifteen all," Mike said softly, not wasting energy on raising his voice. Grunting, he swiped the air at waist level. "Serve," he commanded.

Crystal wanted to rattle his cage again to throw his game off, but was wary of the tense set of his shoulders. Following his directions, she served the ball. It barely skimmed over the net.

"Let ball," he said between clenched teeth.

"It didn't..." she started, but seeing the grinding motion of his lower jaw, stopped before claiming the ball had not touched the net.

"Re-serve," he ordered curtly.

Flustered by his anger, she served the next two into the net.

"Fifteen thirty," she announced before he could. Perspiration beaded on her upper lip. Using the back of her hand, she wiped the moisture away. What had always been a friendly game of tennis was rapidly deteriorating into deadly competition. His competitive spirit she understood, but not this desire to totally annihilate her.

"Hey, boss. Truce. When you stop roaring at me I start looking overhead. Watching for the sky to fall in."

"I'm playing offense," he stated bluntly.

"I'm serving ... you're playing defense," she said, correcting his error in terminology.

"Wrong. When you turn around you'll see why I've been particularly *offensive*."

Bewildered by the grin that suddenly appeared on his face, she followed the direction his racket was pointing. Jane was coming back down the bike path. Nothing unusual about that; she usually joined them at this time.

Crystal's eyes widened. There, riding a ten-speed bike, was Brett Masterson. He was close enough for her to see a racket case perched in the front basket. She felt like groaning. This was not the way she had envisioned starting off a beautiful Saturday morning.

"Finished already?" Jane called, noticing the lack of action.

"No, dear, just pausing for a breather. Hi, Brett. Glad you could join us." His face was wreathed in smiles. "Crystal hasn't been able to concentrate on her game."

The remark directed all attention to Crystal. She wanted to make a witty rejoinder, but her tongue seemed to have become part of the top of her mouth. The theory she had formulated earlier in the week and had attempted to prove was invalid. The lighting here was far different than it had been in the park, but his dark eyes seemed to pick up every last ray and reflect them, much as a mirror reflecting the sun does. Her fingers itched for her camera.

"Crystal thrives on tackling the unconquerable. Maybe your game is rusty and she's bored," Brett suggested with pure devilry in his eyes.

"I beat her regularly," Mike protested, mistaking the jibe at Crystal as a dig at his age.

"Only in the office," Crystal retorted, finally finding her tongue. "How's your game, Brett?"

"Fair to middlin'," he replied while unzipping the carrying case that held his racket.

"Don't let him hustle you, Crystal," Jane interrupted. "He'd be on the pro circuit if his family didn't consider it beneath their dignity."

"Family tree filled with stuffed shirts?" Crystal boldly teased, paying him back for the 'tackling the unconquerable' crack.

"Touché, darling." The endearment brought a heated flush to her face. "Mike, did Crystal tell you that I have something she wants?"

Crystal wanted to run. Every time the horrid man with the fantastic eyes opened his mouth, she felt like flinching.

"Hon, you have something every unmarried female in the three adjoining counties want," Jane said, rolling her eyes to the sky.

"Propositioned you already, has she?" Mike asked with glee.

"Well..." Brett started.

"Crystal's wild about men. Even wanted my picture this morning," Mike teased and bragged simultaneously.

"Mike, unless you would like a freshly typed resignation on your desk Monday morning, and a newly strung racket over your head right now, I suggest you zip your lips." Crystal twirled the steel racket by the neck as she quietly issued the ultimatum.

Both men appeared to be having trouble holding in their laughter. Being the butt of their innuendos rankled Crystal. Her boss was well aware of her attitude toward men, and it wasn't what he was portraying. She saw Jane tugging at Mike's elbow, signaling him to cool it.

"Now, Jane, calm down. Crystal is doing an assignment on what appeals to women, and she wants a picture of my..." Mike paused, realizing what he had been about to disclose. A dark red stain was creeping up his neck.

"Buns," Crystal said, observing his discomfort and completing the sentence for him. Circling around behind her boss, she asked in a low husky voice, "Weren't you attracted by his buns, Jane?"

Now Jane was amused by her husband's blush. "You should see his—"

"Jane, sweetheart, isn't it time for us to be going?" he asked, not letting her finish.

"Just a moment, dear. I want to tell Crystal about..."

"Jane!"

"But, darling, if you're going to let her take a picture and put it in a magazine showing your tush, why can't I tell her about your..."

"Shut up, *dear*." The whisper had the effect of being louder than a cannon.

Crystal glanced at Brett, expecting to see a broad smile on his face. There was no smile. Not even a grin. The corners had a definite downward slant. Holding the racket as a guitarist holds his instrument, Brett silently plucked at the tight strings absentmindedly.

The silence was becoming thick. Mike glared at Jane. Brett self-consciously picked at his racket, and Crystal wanted nothing more than to seclude herself in the privacy of her own apartment.

The irony of the situation was not lost on Crystal. Mike, who had given her the assignment, refused to reveal the intimate detail of what had attracted his wife. Brett, the uptight corporate executive, was reluctant to have his eyes featured in her article and was horrified at the idea of having his older relative's posterior mooning off the glossy pages. And Jane had been reprimanded for telling, or nearly telling, what had attracted her to the man who initially had made the assignment. An unrestrained giggle passed through her lips. The giggle became louder as the faces of the three onlookers displayed shock at her audible reaction to the situation.

Within moments Brett's deep chuckle could be heard, then Mike's laughter, joined by Jane's. Each placed their own interpretation on what had happened, but mutually they agreed, as their mirth mingled, that it was too glorious a morning to waste being angry.

"Mike, you invited me over for a game. I didn't realize what *kind* of a game, but I'd like to have revenge for your duplicity over on the tennis court."

"I'm hardly in your class," Mike replied with restrained modesty, "but I wouldn't mind volleying a few with you."

"Care to join in, Crystal?" Brett asked, turning the full force of his magnetism on her.

"Thanks, but no thanks. I'll enjoy sitting here watching you crucify my boss," she replied smugly, grinning impishly at Mike. "Watch out for his psychological slams," she warned Brett.

The older man raised his racket and started to the far court. Twisting around, he said softly to his wife, "No sharing secrets."

Jane and Crystal smiled at each other. The three words had been directed at both of them. He wanted to beat Brett, but he didn't want to be distracted by having to worry about his wife revealing any information. Jane nodded silently. The nod was a promise.

Watching the two highly competitive men was like viewing a fine ballet performance. Neither man wasted a movement. Brett appeared to flow rather than run from position to position. As he crouched, waiting for the serve, Crystal admired his athletic stature.

He had the grace of a sleek predator. The slight sheen of moisture on his face made his skin glow with a golden tone. At the end of the second set his white tennis shorts were unwrinkled, and there was no telltale sign of stress ringing his armpits.

Why should there be? Crystal mused. Does a sleek jaguar get saggy fur, or sweat profusely when stalking unwary quarry?

The photographer in her surfaced to the top. She had to get pictures of him. What had the lady at the park said? *"Take a picture... it will last longer."* Good advice. The pictures would be around considerably longer than he would be.

Within moments the camera was out of its case and adjusted to the light and distance.

Moving to the net, she snapped picture after picture. Balance, strength, movement, all were captured on film.

No one could appreciate the pictures more than an avid tennis player like herself. Brett would win, of that she was certain. He was, as Mike had commented, in a class by himself.

Stamina was the key. He had paced himself against Mike, knowing the age factor was to his advantage. As Mike slowly began to wear down, Brett came in for the kill. Skillfully, accurately, he placed each ball returned. Poor Mike didn't stand a chance, and he knew it.

Swiftly the game ended. As the two men shook hands over the net, Crystal continued clicking away. She zoomed in, focusing on the hands. One hand short and sprinkled with gray hairs, the other long, firm . . . sensuous.

Momentarily she pictured his hand clasped around her waist, drawing them together. His touch would be as firm as his handshake. The imagined touch sent a teeny tingle up her spine. Turn it off, she silently instructed her rampant imagination. *What would a gorgeous hunk like Brett Masterson want with me?* Ah ha, she thought. *Want* is the operative word. The entire week, both day and night, she had fantasized about Brett, and now, with him only a few feet

away, she mentally completed the dreams....
She wanted him.

Jane strolled past her, drawing her back to
reality. Mike had lost the game, but his wife
rewarded him with a loving embrace.

"Doesn't the victor get a kiss?" Brett asked,
looking directly at Crystal. "It only seems fair."

Letting the camera swing by the neck strap,
Crystal walked to him as though in a daze. If
Brett had been a pro, she would have become a
zealous tennis groupie. Giving him a victory
kiss would be a pleasure... her pleasure.

Her hands felt the smooth muscles of his biceps as they made contact. Standing on tiptoe,
bodies close but not touching, she raised her
lips. Head bent, his eyes changed from the
darkest of browns to a deep black as they liqui-
fied and flowed over her honey-colored gaze.

Brett didn't close his eyes or grab and kiss. He
waited. Crystal thought she felt a tremor in his
arm as she raised her arms and slid them around
his neck, drawing his head down further. Lips
barely touching, she tasted the salt on his
mouth. The tip of her tongue briefly flicked
over his bottom lip before she withdrew. The
tangy salt washed over her taste buds, filling her
mouth with his taste. What appeared to Mike
and Jane as a chaste peck on the mouth was the
most arousing kiss Crystal had ever given.

Mike loudly cleared his throat, making her realize she was in danger of making a complete fool of herself. Stiffening her knees, which had become decidedly weak, Crystal took one step backward.

Brett hadn't moved. He was totally passive. He neither took nor gave. For some unknown reason, this acutely distressed her.

How could he stand there like a bronze statue when she was shaking like a leaf in a windstorm? The attraction is one-sided, she thought. He has had a multitude of glamorous women falling at his feet, and one average, poorly dressed woman was a turnoff, she surmised, covering the hurt with a wry grin. At all costs she wouldn't let him know her reaction to the fleeting kiss. If she did, she knew she would be another notch on his tennis racket.

"How about joining us for breakfast, Crystal?" Jane asked, as she did every Saturday morning after the tennis bout.

"Not this time," Crystal answered with a smile, then turned away, "but thanks for the offer. I'll take a rain check."

"Brett? You're coming, aren't you?" Jane said, glancing from Crystal to Brett with a baffled expression.

"Of course he is," Mike assured his wife.

"Every bachelor welcomes a free, home-cooked meal . . . right, Brett?"

Crystal held her breath, waiting for his reply. She could feel his eyes on her back, but she refused to turn and face him. It was far better for him to go quickly than to linger. The briefer their association, the better.

"Right," Brett finally agreed. "You two go on ahead and I'll pack up my equipment and follow along on my bike."

Jane nudged Mike. Brett wanted to speak to Crystal privately and didn't want an audience. Mike grinned and winked.

"No hurry. Jane makes biscuits and gravy on Saturday morning, and it takes a while. See you, Crystal."

"Bye," Crystal mumbled as she tried to control her shaking fingers enough to pack up her camera and tennis racket.

A prickling sensation at the back of her neck told her Brett was close. Too close for comfort. Where was all the poise she normally had? The tip of her tongue licked her lips, providing the answer. *Back on the tennis court, you fool.* It had slipped, fallen, and shattered when he hadn't returned her kiss.

"If you turned down their invitation because of me, I'm sorry," Brett said, quickly getting to the point.

"Don't be. I don't make a habit of eating with them every Saturday."

"Does my presence make you uncomfortable?" Brett queried.

"Not especially," she lied. "But I don't like people who sneak around making phone calls behind my back."

"Guilty." Brett swung in front of her, blocking the steps taking her off the court. "But not of sneaking or snitching," he added, qualifying the guilty plea. Amusement sparkled in his eyes. "Yes, I inquired about a woman reporter doing a story on male sex appeal. I did *not* mention the day-care story, if that's what you categorize as snitching. Mike did. In fact I was evasive when he asked me if I had been interviewed."

"You lied to Mike?" she asked, doubting his sincerity.

"No. I changed the subject to tennis," he replied, trying valiantly to penetrate the barrier she had erected. "I wanted to see you on a strictly social basis, but I didn't even know if you were engaged or married, or ..."

"Living with a man?" she asked, dodging around his body. "Mike wouldn't know. Private information of that nature is not disclosed in the personnel file."

"Well, are you living with a man?" he directly quizzed, stopping her movement by curving his fingers around her upper arm.

Being touched ignited two conflicting emotions: desire and self-preservation. Desire to be held firmly against the long length of him. Desire to taste his salty lips. Desire to explore beyond the first kiss. The tips of her breasts hardened against the lacy wisps of her bra. Desire flooding through her had passed the mental state and gone on to the aching reality of physical desire.

Self-preservation won as his eyes bore into her threadbare jersey. He knew her thoughts, knew what she was fantasizing. The rounded buds, thrusting up pertly, had betrayed her. An amused, knowing smile flashed over his face, making the laugh creases by his eyes deepen.

He wouldn't humiliate her again, she vowed as self-preservation won the conflict.

"Not one, two," she replied evenly. Not a lie, she thought smugly...a half truth. Scotty and Mac were both male. Male dogs, but nonetheless male. Her lips tilted upward when his hand dropped as though burned. "Artists are known for their loose morals. Why *not* two? Double your pleasure, double your fun!"

"Both of them sleep with you at the same time or do they flip a coin?" he asked in a low growl.

"Usually we sleep together, but sometimes Scotty sleeps on the sofa." Crystal was having difficulty keeping the laughter out of her voice and a full-fledged smile off her face.

"Why should I be shocked?" Brett mumbled to himself. "Any woman who would go around photographing strangers' posteriors isn't all straight."

Anger removed any humor from the conversation. Of all the chauvinistic, priggish remarks, *that* one had to take the cake. The opposite of straight was kinky. She had been given a less-than-straight assignment by *his* relative and it made *her* kinky? She could feel smoke pouring from her ears as anger boiled in her stomach.

"Why don't you go back to your staid family tree...and hang yourself," she suggested through tightly clenched teeth.

Once again Brett moved in front of her, blocking her path. "Since you're an advocate of free love, you won't object to this," he drawled, cupping the nape of her neck with strong fingers.

Having witnessed his superior strength, Crystal expected him to slam his mouth brutally against hers. Averting her head, she tried to avoid a punishing kiss that would leave her lips bruised and sore.

Before a second hand could reach the next

minute marking, she felt firm lips graze against her cheek. The tenseness of his body made her aware of his anger, but his lips were soft... gentle in their supplication as they traveled to the corner of her mouth.

"Let me kiss you," he requested coaxingly.

"No," she said, denying him by twisting her face further away.

His other hand cupped the side of her face, turning and lifting it at the same time. The eyes she had been hypnotized by made any further struggle impossible. Wasn't she getting what she had wanted earlier? Brett was no longer being a passive, bronze statue. He was being the aggressor. The deep coloring of his eyes appealed to her basest instincts.

"Yes!"

Chapter Four

Sweetly, gently, his lips covered hers. Barely moving, they tasted each other. Reality was more delicious than fantasy. The dreams fell short of the actual sensation of his warmth enveloping her. She felt the tip of his tongue, with pointed firmness, outline her lower lip, nibbling, coaxing, begging entrance. Denying herself this one kiss was impossible. Her lips parted.

Deep in his throat he groaned as he pulled her closer, melting them together as he deepened the kiss. With velvet sipping movements, she enticed him, lured him in further. Wanting him to explore all of her sweetness. It was their first, their last, kiss. She wanted it to be the best.

The heat his probing tongue generated was more powerful than the sun. Crystal felt as though her blood had caught fire, making the skin scorching hot.

She lost all sense of time or place. Clasped in his arms, she felt a new, sensuous world had been created. A place lovelier than earth, with colors sparking from the heat, burning with more brilliance than the solar system's brightest star.

"Oh, God, Crystal," Brett murmured, ending the kiss by speaking huskily against her lips. "You'll have to give them up," he moaned, raking his hands over her faded denims, revealing his desire.

"Huh?" she mumbled, insensible to anything other than the loud beating in her chest as heated blood coursed through burning flesh.

"Your lovers," he muttered, planting biting kisses between the words. "Get rid of them. I'm all you need."

The nipping bites chilled her heart, blood, and skin as the meaning of his slanderous words registered. The slender arms she had used to crush them together pushed against his chest. Biting the inside of her lip to detract from the pain his words caused, she tasted a trace of saltiness that eradicated the sweetness she craved.

Brett gripped the soft flesh of her upper arms, restraining her from fleeing. "You can't expect me to move in and make it a four-some," he gritted out, shaking her slightly.

"Why not? The sofa turns into a double bed," she hurled, hiding the anger raging beneath the cool sarcasm.

He no longer disapproved of her supposed loose morals; he wanted a piece of the action! Correction, she thought disgustedly, he wants *all* of the action.

One more violent shake later, he dropped his hands, pivoted, grabbed his tennis equipment, swung his leg over the bike, and rode off. A speeded-up home movie couldn't have moved more jerkily or faster.

Stunned by the kiss, his demand, and the bone-rattling shake, Crystal stood and watched her tormentor pedal off.

"The biggest mistake of my life was taking your picture," she shouted, determined to have the last word. Good riddance to bad rubbish, she fumed, realizing how low his opinion was of her. Belatedly she wished she had kicked his shins or stomped in the spokes of his bike.

When she spied her carryall, her leg swung back, then in midmotion stopped. He wasn't worth the price of a new tennis racket. Inspiration hit! She knew exactly what she would do to relieve her wounded heart. Her foot dropped to the ground and she bent at the waist, hands swooping up her belongings; then her legs strode angrily toward home.

Nonstop she opened the door, dropped the carryall, let the excited dogs in, and slammed into the bedroom she had converted into a darkroom. Under most circumstances she developed film in the darkroom at work, but one roll of film was in urgent need of processing.

Time moved as quickly as her own nimble fingers. Before long she impatiently watched while blank, white paper lying in the bottom of a shallow tray filled with chemicals began developing. The faint line of a blurred figure sharpened.

A smile of accomplishment twisted her lips. Touching the tips of the corners of the picture, Crystal lifted it out of the tray. Using small clips, she hung it on the clothesline in the adjacent dimly lit bathroom. The same sequence was repeated over and over until the line held a double row of dripping pictures of Brett.

The shots were absolutely fantastic—portrait quality. The time spent in the darkroom performing the developing ritual she loved had soothed her temper and modified her intentions. Ripping the images in front of her into tiny shreds suddenly was abhorrent. The quality of the workmanship was too good to be destroyed.

Pointing a finger at the grinning man with shining eyes, she spoke softly. "Brett Masterson, you assume too much. You *assume* that beautiful eyes grant you permission to malign my work. You *assume* personal information from Mike will answer your questions. You *assume* my morals are lax due to my 'artistic temperament.'" Crystal poked the chest of the man in the picture. "You assume too much!"

The muted sound of a ringing door bell took her away from the recriminating monologue taking place in the bathroom. Hurriedly leaving the bathroom she glanced in the full-length mirror at the end of the hall. Long wisps of dark hair had straggled loose from the rubber band around her hair. One sock was up, the other bunched around her ankle.

"Beautiful," she mocked, using one hand to tuck the fly-away hair behind her ear and the other to pull up the sagging sock.

The ringing became incessant. One peal after another in rapid succession. Scotty and Mac joined in the cacophony with high-pitched yips.

"Hush, dogs," she called, reprimanding them sharply, grabbing Scotty by the collar to keep him from dashing out the door.

"Who's there?"

"Florist for Crystal Lake."

"Hang on a minute."

Crossing the living room, she called the dogs
to the sliding patio door and shooed them out.

"If you're going to be rowdy," she scolded,
"stay outside."

Retracing her steps, she swung the front
door wide open, expecting to see a uniformed
teenager from the local florist. Her honey-
colored eyes widened. Brett thrust a yellow tulip from her own flower bed toward her.

"May I come in?"

Crystal's left arm moved to slam the door in
his face. A strong shoulder prevented that from
happening.

"No. Stay out of here!" she said, and gasped,
stiffening her arms and pushing harder.

Brett, being physically stronger, inched the
door open and stepped between the door and
the frame. Inside the apartment he advanced;
Crystal retreated. The grim, clamped lips made
a straight slash. His eyes were pebble hard.
Hands clenched, he silently strode toward her.

The space between them widened when he
stopped. Crystal felt her heels touching the
paneling of the back wall in the entry. She was
trapped. Trapped in her own home with a
maniac intent on foul play. Her overactive
imagination flashed the plots of several murder
mysteries before her eyes.

Reacting the way she had been instructed to

do in a threatening situation, Crystal screamed, *"Fire!"*

"Shut up," Brett ground out, clamping his hand over her mouth as the high-pitched wail rent through the apartment.

Twisting, squirming, futilely kicking at his shins, she felt herself being firmly but gently restrained.

"Don't do it," she heard before sinking her teeth into the palm of his hand. "Calm down, wildcat. I'll let you go when you promise not to scream."

"Let go of me," she insisted, indistinctly pounding her fists against his rib cage.

She could hear the dogs yipping and scratching at the patio door. Surely the neighbors would know something was amiss and rescue her. This hope renewed her physical efforts to escape. The sound of him sharply sucking in air as she elbowed his ribs was better than hearing applause at an art gallery.

His head jerked toward the glass doors. Crystal felt herself being hauled in that direction and dug her heels into the thick green carpet. His superior strength outmatched her determination to leave the raucous pets outside to attract attention.

Brett spun her around, hand still clamped on her mouth, and spoke softly to the terriers,

"It's okay, Scotty. Down, Mac." Both dogs quit yelping simultaneously.

Back pressed against his chest, Crystal tilted her head and saw her watchdogs wagging their tails, joyously licking at his pants leg.

"Some protectors you are!" she complained into the hand gagging her. "Attack!"

Hooking his leg behind the bend of her knees, Brett caved her toward him and toppled to the floor, bearing the brunt of her falling weight without breaking contact. A sharp grunt as they hit the floor was the only noise she heard before having her face washed by dog tongues.

"Yuck," she mumbled into his hand, shaking her head to make the dogs stop.

Rolling her onto her back, he imprisoned the lower third of her kicking legs with his strongly muscled thigh. Her wrists were manacled by one large hand and strung high above her head. A curious warmth spread over her at the intimate contact of his body.

"This one is from your lover Scotty," Brett mumbled, removing his hand and replacing it with his mouth in a swift, brief kiss. "Mac gets equal treatment," he whispered. The second kiss was little more than a hard peck. "And one for me."

The last kiss began furiously, but abruptly changed to gentle softness.

Crystal fought the first two by wiggling, scrunching, and twisting her head. The third quieted her struggles. The heated physical bout, the friction of their clothes rubbing against each other, brought an awareness of more than male strength. She found herself responding, opening her lips to deepen the kiss.

Subconsciously she regretted having misled Brett into believing she lived with two men. Consciously she wondered if she had masochistic tendencies. *No.* Angry kisses had kept her fighting; gentle persuasion was defeating her. She felt Brett shudder when he deepened the kiss further. The effect they had on each other was mutual surrender.

A third nose, cold and wet, nuzzled between their faces. Eyes opening, Crystal saw two small dark orbs, closer than the smoldering, larger, darker eyes.

"Scotty...Mac...meet Brett Masterson," she quipped, smiling as she introduced Brett to his rivals. All the fight had dissipated with what could have developed into a devastating flare of passion.

"No more *fire*?" Brett asked, brushing her curved lips before easing away and releasing her hands.

"Not one I'd want the neighbors to put out," she replied honestly.

A wry smile brought a lopsided grin to his face. "A few more blows to the rib cage, and I'd have needed the medics. You aren't an only child...that's for certain. Did your brothers win any of the fights?" he inquired in a teasing voice.

"He gave up trying before we were teen-agers."

"One brother? Younger or older?"

"Older."

"Sisters?"

"One. Younger."

"Names?"

"Gus and Windy."

Crystal knew he was connecting the last name and her mother's choice of first names.

"Windy Lake I get, but Gus Lake?" he asked with a chuckle.

"Gus is short for Gusty," she replied with a girlish giggle.

"I'm afraid to ask about middle names," he rejoined.

"They are worse. I'm Crystal Clare; Gus is named after Dad...Storm Gusty Lake; and Windy Gail Lake," she said, groaning with him as she revealed the names on the family birth certificates.

"How could your mother do that to innocent babes?" Brett inquired.

"Simple. Any other type of name would have made the child an outcast. Mom's name is..." Crystal giggled again, deliberately pausing when she saw the light of anticipation in his eyes. "Serena... get it? Serene Lake."

Lying back on the carpet, Brett chuckled softly and was rewarded with a sloppy lick from Mac. Picking the dog up and placing him on his chest, Brett said to the dog in a confidential manner, "No wonder she's a fighter."

Mac yipped once, bounding away to stretch out beside Scotty, who was sprawled in the sunshine coming through the sliding glass doors.

Propping himself back up on one elbow, Brett's eyes slowly meandered over the freckles on her nose. "They're like gold dust. I'd like to kiss each one," he murmured close to her ear.

"Gold dust? Stars? You're very poetic. Any writers in your family?" Crystal was as curious about his background as he had been over hers. She knew he was related to Mike and that pro tennis was beneath the dignity of his family, but, at best, that was sketchy information.

"Writers?" he replied mockingly. "My parents would be appalled at the thought. The Masterson family can be traced on both sides, back to the Civil and Revolutionary wars." An eyebrow raised aristocratically, he peered down his aquiline nose at Crystal. "And I'm not re-

ferring to those minor skirmishes you colonists call wars."

Crystal stroked his cheek with a swift pat, then sat up Indian-style, legs hooked into each other. Looking down at him, she mocked, "Poor little rich boy?"

"There is nothing poor about being a Masterson," he chided, running a fingertip over one of her knees. "Don't start feeling sorry for me. There's no need. Wealth isn't restrictive; it's liberating."

"Humph!" Crystal snorted. "Mike said you couldn't play pro tennis."

"Are you aware you communicate like a black-and-white negative? You're stereotyping," he commented sagely, trailing the straying finger higher up her inner thigh.

Slapping his hand, she sniffed indignantly. "Would you care to explain that remark, or shall I hit you with the family crest?"

Playfully, hiding behind his arms, he said, "No more brawling, please. I'm black and blue already." Levering himself up, he copied her sitting position. Knees touching, he bent forward, taking her hands, lacing their fingers.

"Let's review the facts: I don't want my picture in print. I'm a corporate executive. My family is old money." Mechanically he ticked off the facts as Crystal nodded her head.

"Therefore, I'm a pin-striped, spanking clean stuffed shirt." He tightened the grip on her fingers perceptibly, knowing her reaction to his summation would be withdrawal.

Doing the unexpected, Crystal squeezed them tighter. "Aren't you?"

"No. Should I diagnose your problem as having a severe case of inverse snobbery?"

"Practicing medicine without a license?" she retorted glibly. "If I have this obvious flaw in my character, why did you ring my door bell?"

"Because, my dear, you have spiked my guns in every minor skirmish we have had. You may be allowed to win a few battles, but I'm going to win the war," he declared confidently.

"And what are the spoils of victory?" she asked, using his war terminology.

A wide grin fanned the tilting creases beside his eyes. "Total capitulation. You'll be my prisoner."

The vague answer did not satisfy her black-and-white personality. Losing a war was synonymous with defeat, as was capitulation. Was she going to accept the fate he had deemed the final outcome? *Absolutely not.* Tugging her hands, she tried to effect an immediate release from the physical hold he had on her.

"Before you resume the hostilities, you ought to decide what you're fighting for . . . or against," he cautioned, spreading his fingers apart abruptly. "And now that I've temporarily released you, can we arbitrate a truce?"

"Armed?" she asked, enjoying his wit.

"No other way," he replied, raking her from chin to toes, an admiring glance lingering on the long, silken legs the brief shorts displayed. "Your weapons are formidable."

"You could concede now and honorably withdraw your forces," she quipped.

Easing himself to his feet, he offered his hand down to Crystal. "Normally I adhere to the philosophy of being a lover rather than a fighter. In your case"—she had placed her slender hand in his—"I'll reverse the concept." In slow motion he elevated her off the floor. "I'll fight to win your love."

How is that for bold, black-and-white ten-inch lettering? she mused silently, staring up into his magnetic dark eyes. His arsenal wasn't empty either!

A spark of humor made her counter wickedly, "I'd hate to contemplate being a loser by loving you."

"I'll ignore that," he said, parrying her thrust. "How about peace talks while having K-rations?"

"Certainly a unique way of inviting a girl out for lunch," she commented, reaching down to pet Mac. The terrier thumped his stubby tail and sighed blissfully as she scratched his tummy. "I'll have to change clothes."

Brett intently watched her stroke the dog. The wistful expression on his face reminded her of a small boy rather than a mighty warrior— with his face pressed against the window of a pet store.

"He loves having his belly rubbed," she said, stating the obvious.

"I can empathize with that," he said candidly, winking. "I was envying the dog."

"Wrong one," she said, smiling and giving Mac a final thump. "He sleeps on the sofa."

Shaking his head, Brett headed toward the front door. "Win or lose, the Battle of Wits will be anything but dull," he said dryly. "I'll be back in an hour."

Bending, he picked up the tulip he had dropped earlier. The bloom drooped on its limp stem.

"Next time we'll put the flowers in water before you throw me on the floor," he teased. Breaking off the majority of the stem, he touched his fingertip to the yellow stamen in the dark center and rubbed the pollen between his fingers. Pushing her hair back, he tucked the flower behind her ear.

"Did I just witness a secret warriors' ritual?" she interrogated lightly.

A dark stain crept up his neck. "You're far too observant."

"Well...explain," she demanded, watching his ears tinge slightly pink.

"A general doesn't reveal his secret weapons until he wins the war, but I'll give you a clue: luck."

Sliding a finger under the thin chain encircling her neck, Crystal hooked a small ivory charm from beneath her tank top.

"My talisman wards off all hexes, curses, and potions."

Taking the exquisitely carved ivory from between her fingers, Brett carefully examined it. Each detail, from flowing mane and tail to the tiny hooves, was meticulously crafted.

"White Horse Luck, we call it. Each member of the family has one," she said with pride.

The knuckles of his hand nestled against the upper swell of her breasts. A tiny shiver made the hairs rise on her arms. Brett slowly released the charm. Eyes glowing, he paused, seemingly regretting its absence in the warmth of his palm.

Taking a deep breath, he said as he opened the door, "An hour?"

"Forty-five minutes," she bargained, dreading his departure.

Eyes smiling, a mixed look of satisfaction and anticipation splashed over his features.

Crystal reflected the same emotions as she watched him stride toward his bike. His hands in the pockets of his tennis shorts stretched the white fabric tightly across rounded muscles.

"Good buns," she murmured.

Scotty, the escape artist, eager to get out of the apartment, tried to wriggle between her legs and the door frame.

"Down, boy," she reprimanded, quickly shutting the door. The long-haired black dog quirked his head to one side and whimpered.

"None of that. I'll take you and Mac for a run later," she promised as she crossed into the bedroom.

Happily she rubbed her hands together. She hadn't been this excited about a date in years. Questions she had not asked herself in ages popped into her mind. Did Brett feel the same way? Hand over her heart, she could feel it thud as adrenaline pumped through her system. What should I wear? Where will he take me for K-rations? The broad grin expanded into a full-blown chuckle of glee.

Time to gloat later, Crystal ole girl. Right now you have some major repair work to do on your appearance.

Quickly she strode into the bathroom. Darn, she thought, glancing into the mirror over the lavatory, my hair is a disaster. It needs to be washed. Brett's face appeared to be looking over her shoulder.

"The first thing I have to do is remove the present occupant of the shower!"

Agile fingers pinched the clips releasing the photos. Stacking the photos on a shelf in the darkroom, she recalled her previous plan of revenge and laughed. Sheer folly, she thought. By using them in her article she would have jeopardized more than a lawsuit. It would have exposed Brett to the speculative eyes of all the women in St. Louis. Silently she admitted to herself she didn't want him to be the recipient of any fan mail the article would provoke.

Rushing, Crystal showered, shampooed, and dressed within half an hour. After applying a light coat of cosmetics and dressing in snug navy-blue slacks with matching silky blue blouse, she plugged in the hair blower and began combing her waist-long hair. Only the tips were damp when the door bell rang and the dogs commenced barking.

"He's early," she commented to Mac, who was dashing between the bedroom and the front door. It delighted her to think he was as anxious to start the afternoon as she was.

Swinging the door open, she was startled to

see Chad. He had been to a few parties she had given, but never had he dropped by uninvited.

"Mike sent me," he said, explaining his unexpected arrival.

"Why?" she asked, further bewildered by the reason for his inopportune arrival. Courteously she motioned for Chad to enter.

"Someone put a bug in the boss's ear about your photographing male butts," he answered crudely with a disdainful expression. "I've been instructed to tag along for this part of the assignment." Chad walked into the living room and flung himself horizontally on the sofa.

"Terrific," she commented. "Get your feet off my couch." Twisting a length of hair over her shoulder, she debated whether to spend the day with Chad working or stick to the impromptu plan of going out with Brett.

"I'd rather work on the assignment tomorrow. I've made plans for today. Anyway, what's the rush?"

"No rush. Mike knew you'd be working, regardless of the day of the week, and sent me over to supervise the operation." The implication that Crystal was his assistant rather than vice versa was distressing.

Having Chad lord it over her was more infuriating than the feet that remained on her sofa.

The urge to kick his skinny rear end right out of her home and damn the consequences made her dig her fingernails into the palms of her hands.

"Mike may have sent you over to tag along, but he wouldn't send you here to supervise my work. You and I both know I'm quite capable of completing the assignment . . . without male interference." The insult was blatantly clear.

"The *boss* said," Chad began in a belligerent tone as the door bell pealed.

"Excuse me," Crystal broke in, welcoming the distraction.

Her heart pounded a little faster, a little louder, as the same gleam she had photographed entered Brett's eyes as they swept over her. The flush on her high cheekbones deepened attractively.

"Come in," she bade in a lowered voice. "Complications have arisen since you left."

Preceding Crystal toward the living room, Brett halted at the doorway. Chad had remained lounging comfortably on the sofa, and acknowledged his presence with a slight lift of one hand. He acted as though he was the guest and Brett the intruder.

"Chad is the other photojournalist at *SLC*," she said, both introducing and explaining his presence. "Mike thought I was going to work today and suggested Chad play the role of psuedobodyguard." A forced laugh did not relieve the tension in the room.

"Hon, you know I'll be more than a bodyguard," he replied suggestively as his eyes focused on the twin peaks of her breasts. "We'll be . . . partners. Working together closely, as we always do."

Crystal wasn't fooled by the double entendre or the hint that they had more than a professional relationship. He was intentionally making trouble. The size of their office was the thin strain of truth that made the insinuation a believable lie. She could see Chad's jibe being swallowed by Brett, who then became tense, thrusting his jaw forward as he visually sized up what he thought was his competition. Crystal's back molars ground together as both men looked at her as though she were some sort of prize.

"Chad, you'll have to leave," she ordered abruptly. "Call me in the morning and we'll make arrangements to shoot some pictures at one of the sporting events."

"Athletic buns are best?" Chad inquired with a crooked grin meant to be engaging but falling flat when it met the tightly compressed lips and the strong jaw of Brett's face.

"We'll discuss it tomorrow," Crystal warned, eager to remove his offensive presence.

Bending at the waist, Chad swung his feet to the floor and stood, shaking his head negatively. Brett towered over him. Crystal could sense the tightly leashed control Brett was exerting to keep his temper in check. It was imperative to get rid of Chad quickly; then she would tackle Brett herself. She was discovering a violent side to her nature regarding both men. She could cheerfully draw and quarter Chad for constantly being a pain in the ... buns, and Brett contacting Mike was doubly infuriating.

Mutely crossing to the door, she escorted Chad out.

"See you tomorrow."

"I'll bet you don't stamp REJECTED on his underwear," Chad muttered for her ears only as he walked out.

Crystal shut the door and spun around at the same time. Bright red flags of anger heralded her intentions. Brett raised both hands, arms straight out, to avoid any physical lashing out. Amusement flickered in his dark eyes.

"Truce?" he quipped.

"Open warfare! Where do you get off discussing my work with Mike?" she fired.

Approaching her cautiously, he replied softly, "I mentioned the possibility of your being placed in a compromising situation to Mike. My intentions were strictly honorable. That pipsqueak"—one hand gestured toward the door—"will cause more problems than he will prevent. I'll escort you myself," he volunteered.

The thought of having Brett follow along, carrying her equipment and asking for signatures, intrigued Crystal. Or was the possibility of being with him both Saturday and Sunday the sole attraction?

A wide smile erased the scowl. "You'll have to do exactly what I tell you to do. I'll be the officer in charge of operations," she stipulated before acquiescing.

Groaning, Brett closed the gap between them and placed his arm over her shoulder. "I have a feeling you are maneuvering me toward an ignoble defeat, but if that is my punishment for trying to protect you, so be it."

"You'll follow my orders explicitly?" she questioned incredulously, touching the hand dangling over her shoulder dangerously near the fabric tautly stretching over her breasts.

"Like a raw recruit. However, I expect to be lured into service. You can work on that today."

"You're prime material for officer's train-

ing," she complimented, squeezing his fingertips.

"Be careful," he warned huskily. "Soldiers
are billeted near their commanding officer."

A teeny electrical charge shot from her fingertips to her heart. The double entendres were
being fired with deadly accuracy. Crystal arched
her head back, smiling. His sensuous lips,
spreading in a grin, promised an exciting week-
end. As they lowered Crystal felt the exhil-
aration a soldier must feel when facing battle.
Rising on tiptoes to meet the oncoming force,
she reminded herself to remain unconquerable.
Her heart knew war games could leave her in-
jured and bleeding unless she kept her forces
on guard. Each time he kissed her, she felt her
defenses being outflanked.

Earlier he had questioned what she was fighting for or against. Held closely, the kiss deepening, Crystal couldn't remember more than her
name, rank, and serial number: Crystal Clare
Lake, photojournalist, number two . . . and trying harder.

Chapter Five

"No more diversionary tactics," Brett growled against Crystal's ear as his hands roamed over her silky blouse.

"You're banning kisses as ammunition?" she inquired.

"I'm banning the use of imaginary troops such as Scotty and Mac." Licking, then nipping the lobe of her ear, he tortured her senses.

"You accused me of stereotyping, then did the same thing yourself," she accused softly, defending her ploy. "I merely confirmed your reconnaissance." Her arms stole up and around the strong column supporting his head.

"They were a decoy, and you know it," he replied, spreading his fingers, feeling the texture of her hair. "If Mike hadn't rolled on the floor with laughter when I inquired about your live-in boyfriends, I would have been over here on a seek-and-destroy mission." Deep laughter rumbled in his chest, vibrating against her breasts. "You're devious, but delightful."

"Starvation is against the Geneva Code," she broadly hinted, turning toward the door.

"Brainwashing is too, but my strategy is to erode your defenses by kissing you every fifteen seconds." Dropping a chaste kiss on her forehead, he nudged her out the door toward a silver Cadillac.

"Some jeep," Crystal commented, grinning.

Lightheartedly they bantered back and forth as Brett drove. He used every stop sign and traffic light as an excuse to practice his brainwashing technique. Crystal found herself pressing her right foot down to brake the car when she spotted a green light. The playful camaraderie, his quick wit, and braking the car, kept her on her toes.

Realizing she had no idea where they were going other than heading north on Lindbergh, she asked, "What kind of K-rations are we having?"

"There is a Mexican restaurant in Westport I'm partial to. Any objections?"

"None. I love tacos."

"I love . . . things hot, and spicy," he replied, firing a devastating grin at her during the pause. "Their chalupas are better than any north of the Texas state line. Stop sign!'' Leaning over, he brushed her lips with a featherlike kiss. ''Mmmmm. Better than jalapeños.''

''What's a chalupa? And why Texas instead of the Mexican border?''

''One question at a time,'' he protested, laughing. ''A chalupa is a fried-flour tortilla, piled high with refried beans, meat, hot sauce, lettuce, tomatoes, and guacamole.''

''Sounds like a taco with green gooey stuff instead of cheese.''

''Chalupas are better.'' Fingertips touching his lips, he made the typically French gesture for excellence. ''But the absolute best are served in Texas.''

''Did you vacation in Texas?'' she inquired, picking up tidbits of information about his past.

''I was transferred to Dallas for three years. Last summer I spent two weeks in the sun on Padre Island. Missouri is home, though. My roots are here.''

Turning left on Page Avenue, Crystal saw the towering golden glass skyscraper ahead. Westport shopping center contained a variety of shops and restaurants that were a blend of ultramodern on the south end, and Swiss chalet architecture to the north. Outside of the Clayton area, it had the best restaurants in St. Louis County.

Seated in a bright red booth side by side, Crystal and Brett studied the menu. Her entire repertoire of Spanish food was taco, tamale, and enchilada. Two of the three were attempts to vary her diet in the frozen food section of the grocery store. Reading the descriptions printed under the foreign words, her midwest palate began to water.

When she turned to ask Brett to recommend what she should order, she completely forgot about food when she saw the intent look on his face as he studied her dark hair falling over her shoulder, honey-colored eyes, and smiling mouth. A younger, less experienced woman would have blushed under the intensity of his penetrating gaze. Crystal smiled even wider.

"What do you suggest?"

"Leaving," he murmured into her ear provocatively.

"Without any K-rations?" she teased, tilting her face a few scant inches from his.

"I'm not contemplating food at the moment. I'm contemplating..."

"Telling me all about yourself?" she impishly guessed.

Brett shook his head negatively.

"Helping me choose what I'm going to eat?" she guessed again.

The intense look vanished. A crooked grin

replaced it. "I'm contemplating ordering for you and seeing your face turn beet red as you call me a chauvinist." Amusement danced in his eyes wickedly.

"I'd appreciate your kindness," Crystal said, unexpectedly demure. Dunking a chip into the green sauce in the center of the table, she popped it into her mouth.

If eyes could light up, spin around, and pop out, Crystal's would have. The innocuous sauce was liquid nitrogen. Tears streamed down her face in an effort to put out the fire raging in her mouth. *What do I do now? Spit or swallow?* Gulping it down before it could permanently damage her tongue, she tried to douse the inferno by draining a glass of ice water. One wasn't enough. Reaching over Brett, unaware of the laughter he was smothering with a napkin, she grabbed his water. The second glass of water tempered the flames, but didn't totally extinguish the fire.

"You knew!" The words were strangled out hoarsely.

A chip between his fingers, Brett dipped it into the avocado and jalapeño sauce, put it in his mouth, and chewed it as though thoroughly savoring the taste.

Crystal was amazed. Does he have steel-plating over his taste buds? she wondered. He must!

"Delicious," he said, rubbing salt into her burning wound. Shoveling up sauce on another chip, he offered it to her.

"It takes a little getting used to. Try again?" Amused eyes smiled at her.

"My tongue has third-degree burns," she laughingly complained. "How do you eat that stuff?"

Chuckling, he replied, "It's like love. The first time you're badly burned. Then you're wary. Finally you acquire a taste for it." Winking broadly, he shoveled the sauce on a curled chip and neatly poked it into his mouth.

"Were you badly burned?" Crystal asked, eating a chip with no sauce.

"I've never been married. Does that answer your question?"

"I guess. Judging by the way you're inhaling that molten lava, you must have acquired a taste for it."

Brett didn't reply verbally. He smiled broadly, showing both rows of even white teeth.

Crystal's heart did a flip-flop. How could any woman resist him? She'd have to try. Acquiring a taste for Brett Masterson could cause terminal heartburn.

A young waiter, obviously of Spanish descent, approached the booth to take their order. "*Bueños dias, amigos.* May I take your order?"

A raised eyebrow silently inquired as to who would make the selection.

With a cheeky smile Crystal said, "I'm wary, but willing to acquire a taste. You do the honors, but keep in mind, the roof of my mouth is in danger of collapsing."

Fluent in Spanish, Brett conversed with the waiter. She could tell they were discussing more than what was on the menu by the amount of laughter being exchanged. When the aromatic food arrived, she was pleasantly surprised. Cautiously tasting small bites of each dish, she discovered it to be spicy but mild.

Brett was utterly charming. Mixing amusing anecdotes about his past with humorous comments about the present, he provided her with more than the K-rations he had promised.

Replete with the meal, Crystal sank back into the cushions as she savored the Mexican coffee with real whipped-cream topping Brett had ordered instead of a dessert.

How many times during the meal she had wished for her camera. Clad in brown slacks and a blue and beige plaid shirt, he made a handsome picture. During the meal she had been aware of other eyes watching him. The magnetic pull he exuded made others want to be near him, be a part of his conversation. Charisma. The special quality that made a mere man magnificent was an inherent part of him. His attention had been directed solely toward her with such intensity, it had made her throat close on several occasions. Crystal was convinced that had the most voluptuous woman in St. Louis paraded naked, strumming a guitar, Brett would not have noticed. He only had eyes for her. More than any words spoken, or any compliments given, that fact made her feel... cherished.

"Ready?" Brett asked when she finished her coffee.

The few moments of daydreaming made her response revealing. "Ready, willing, and able."

After paying the bill and leaving the restaurant, they strolled hand in hand back toward the car. As he courteously helped her into the car, she couldn't help the perpetual smile curving her lips. Brett, she acknowledged ruefully, was the type of man she could fall for ... hard.

Who are you kidding? she mused. You're already falling, and have been since the first picture in the park. Surprisingly, it didn't bother her. In fact, realizing she was on the verge of falling in love made her skin tingle.

Lost in happy thoughts, she jumped when

Brett picked her hand off the leather seat and traced her love line with the tip of his tongue. Drawn by his hooded eyes, she moved closer and saw desire lighting them. Locking her fingers around his thumb, she drew his hand to the side of her face, turning her lips to kiss the warm palm. The callouses formed from gripping more than a pencil lightly raked against her glowing cheek.

"Crystal . . . Crystal," she heard before he buried his face in the crook of her neck. "Necking in the middle of the day in a parking lot is neither the time nor the place, but . . ." The hand she had kissed tilted her head toward his waiting lips.

The light, teasing kisses she had delighted in couldn't compare with the hungry passion of his questing mouth. Returning the kiss, twisting closer, she felt a desire building faster than a flashbulb exploding before her eyes. The same vivid colors burst behind her eyelids. She drew him more deeply into their embrace and the bursting lights divided and multiplied as he hauled her onto his lap. Breasts flattened against his chest, she seemed to be melting, flowing over him, but wanting more.

Brett ended the kiss. Not abruptly, but with great reluctance. The smoldering darkness of his eyes gleamed brightly. Crystal felt them scorching her face, then settling on her slightly swollen lips. She knew he was making a decision. One she should influence, but couldn't. Cradled in his arms she could no more reverse the fates than stop photochemicals from changing a blank sheet of paper into a colorful picture. The first flutterings of love had made her heart beat faster; the passionate kiss made it pound inside her chest.

She saw him close his eyes and squeeze them tightly, signaling his decision. Sliding back across to her side of the front seat, she cast him a half-hearted smile.

"Explosive, isn't it?"

"Lethally," he replied tersely, raising his hips while pulling and straightening the pants fabric over bunched muscles. "I'm going to avoid temptation next time."

Starting the car, he backed out of the parking space, then drove to the parking lot exit. Crystal couldn't deny tempting him, but the words and his tone of voice hurt. Couldn't he tell she had been deeply affected by their burst of passion? Did the starch in his shirt extend below his belt buckle? Starched underwear had to be uncomfortable, she thought, laughing to herself.

The grim expression on his face and the muscle ticking by the curve of his jaw made her contain the laugh. He had declared war on her emotions, but appeared to be struggling with an internal battle.

Outrageously she suggested, grinning broadly, "Why don't we unilaterally agree to an armistice?"

His jaw slackened in surprise as his head swiveled in her direction. "You'll marry me?" he rumbled in disbelief.

"Marry?" she squeaked, hand bracing herself against the dashboard. "That's a bit drastic, isn't it?"

"I can't... *won't* discuss this while driving. Marshal your forces, my captain, you are about to be attacked on the home front."

Glancing at the speedometer, Crystal expected to see it sway to the right, but the white indicator remained steadily below the speed limit. Disliking the tense silence, she twisted the chrome knob by her left knee. The quadraphonic sound brought the multiple-stringed melody of classical music into the car interior.

Music to soothe the savage breast, she noted before changing the station, was not her goal. She wanted him to totally lose control. Lordy, Lordy, she thought, switching the station back to its original setting. *I need to calm down more than he thinks he does. I'm on the verge of throwing caution to the wind, of being totally reckless.*

Neither of them spoke until they were seated in her apartment. The cool green warmth of the decor and the exuberant welcome of Scotty and Mac stopped the tumultuous feelings Crystal had felt when she had opened the door. Keeping the upper hand and remaining in control of her rampant tongue was possible in the confines of her own established territory.

Gesturing toward the well-stocked bar, she asked Brett if he would like a drink.

"Scotch would be fine," he answered, leaning his head back on the plush cushion of the flowered sofa.

Crystal opened the decanter of Chivas Regal and poured a shot glass to the brim. "Ice?"

"Please."

Moving into the kitchen, she filled a lowball glass with ice, then returned to the portable bar and poured in the Scotch. Although her throat was becoming increasingly dry, she did not fix herself a drink. The last thing she needed to do was befuddle her mind with alcohol.

Handing Brett the drink, she was careful not to touch his fingers. Shooing Mac out of the high-backed wing chair beside the fireplace, she gracefully seated herself. Mac grunted his displeasure and jumped on the sofa next to Brett. He snuggled along the length of his leg and sighed at his mistress as his head rested high on

Brett's thigh. Immediately Crystal wished she could exchange places.

A grin and a raised eyebrow told her Brett was aware of the wistful expression on her face. The eyebrow dropped as she grinned and shrugged her shoulders.

"What about marriage?" The baldness of the question was softened by the gentleness in which it was asked.

"Impossible. We hardly know each other," she replied, smoothing the nap of velveteen on the arm of the chair in one direction and then back again. Its soft roughness reminded her of the texture of his cheeks. The thought made her hand still.

"What's to know that can't be discovered later?" he asked logically.

"Plenty."

"Such as?"

Crystal's finger circled the piping. Why did he want a lifetime commitment on such short acquaintance? Or did he consider marriage with the attitude that if it works out fine, and if it doesn't, let the divorce courts handle it. Divorce! Here the man had barely asked her to marry him, and she was negatively anticipating the probability of divorce.

"Why not a less permanent arrangement?" she suggested, her thoughts reflected in the question.

Moving Mac's head, Brett stood. He paced the length of the room once. Hands on lean hips, he replied staunchly, "No." Raking one hand over his head to the loose collar at his neck, Crystal noticed he rubbed it as though a headache or tense muscles were bothering him.

"Want an aspirin?" she offered.

"No. I want you," he answered tersely, then added, "but not on a temporary basis." Lowering his hand, he hooked his thumb into his belt. "Living together isn't my style. I want to know that when I wake up in the morning, you'll always be there. I want to know that when I've had a rough day and I'm not feeling charming or gallant, you'll be there, and you'll wash away my weariness. I want to know you'll believe in me, trust me, even if you are hurt or angry. None of that comes with an affair. I need a commitment."

"Isn't that supposed to be the woman's line?" Crystal asked, chuckling, trying to bring levity into their discussion. "Followed by, if you have your way with me tonight you won't respect me in the morning?"

Brett's laughter concealed his intent as he crossed to the chair and scooped her into his arms. In three long strides he was back to the sofa, turned, and seated with Crystal held firmly on his lap.

"Better," he said, kissing her swiftly. "I'm

going to get beneath the coat of laughter you arm yourself with. By all rights I should be livid with you for laughingly rejecting my proposal. I should be holding you *over* my knee instead of *on* my knee.'' His lips skimmed over her temple to the soft spot behind her earlobe. ''You win this battle, but keep in mind, eventually I will have total surrender.''

''Your blitzkrieg didn't work,'' she retorted, eyes twinkling. One nail circled his outer ear in the same rounded configuration she had used on the edge of the chair. Tilting her head toward the closed door of her bedroom, she said brazenly, knowing he would refuse, ''Care to...''

The offer was smothered and eaten by his lips, boldly suggesting the bedroom was wicked. Surprisingly she felt safer than she ever had. For years she had fought off the physical advances of men who thought a young, attractive woman living alone was fair game. Brett's hand sliding up and down her spine didn't make her want to fight him off, even when it slipped around to cup the underside of her full breast. Confidently she knew he would stop before he lost control.

Eyes closed, the musky odor of aftershave filled her nostrils. The sound of silk caressing the lacy wisps of her bra was arousing the tips of her breasts. There was no fear in her heart when she darted her tongue back and forth between his lips provocatively while unbuttoning his shirt.

The contrast in texture between the smoothly trimmed hair at the nape of his neck, and its coarser, darker mate on his muscular chest was subtly, sensuously different. Their mouths, hair, and hands mingled and stroked. The closer they came, the more they touched, the brighter the fires of passion flamed. Neither was content with the restrictive clothing hampering their private investigation of each other. As if communicating without words, only by touch, they swiftly shed their shirts.

Crystal didn't know whether she had removed her own clothing or his, but a ripple of joy spread through her as she gripped the taut skin covering the muscles on his shoulders and back. No longer on his lap, but stretched out beside him on the sofa, she eased the ache at the juncture of her thighs by capturing his long leg between hers. She could feel the heat of his mouth breathing its moisture on her flushed skin as he kissed and licked his way to the rosy crescents turgidly awaiting his lips.

Breathing raggedly into his hair, she arched as his tongue circled around the dark center. The tip puckered invitingly. A sensation close to pain coursed downward as his lips pulled it into the heat of his mouth, raking it gently with the edge of his teeth. Caressing, clenching, rubbing against his thigh, she eased the delightful ache.

"Brett," she murmured hoarsely, repeatedly.

No longer was her mind concerned with safety. Passion and desire ruled. She couldn't hear the endearments and words of praise Brett mumbled against her skin. Wantonly she drew his leg intimately against the hot core of her womanhood.

Feeling the bulge of his desire between his thighs excited her further, taking her to a higher peak. The control Brett constantly displayed, the strong will, was succumbing to the age-old rite as he thrust against her, rocking them back and forth.

Unsatisfied with stroking his head, shoulders, and back, Crystal slowly lowered her hands to the buckle on the belt surrounding his trim waist. Pulling the leather loose from the metal clasp, she began lowering the zipper, touching the cloth confining his straining manhood.

"No," she heard Brett pant, pulling away slightly.

"No? Yes, Brett," she coaxed, unwilling to

continue the pleasuring of her body without giving an equal amount of physical pleasure to him. Her hand closed over him. "Yes," she repeated huskily, stroking.

Rising over her, Brett demanded she open her eyes. Heavily the lids parted.

"Stop," he commanded, not accepting her refusal.

Confused by the verbal order conflicting with the desire gleaming in his eyes, her hand stopped. She discerned the effort it took him to withdraw from the circle of love her arms had made around his waist. It was truly a test of mental power over physical desires. Her insight into his struggle helped alleviate the ache she felt when he slowly shifted his weight from the sofa and kneeled beside her.

His dark expressive eyes showed tenderness as he eased the silk shirt back over her slender shoulders. Starting at the bottom he began pushing the buttons closed.

"I can't deny the obvious. I want you," he said, speaking ever so softly, "but I want to be more than a male body. Between us, it has to be more than . . . lust."

"You—"

"Shhhh," he said, hushing her interruption. "I've pushed too hard, too fast." Closing the last button, he brushed his lips against the valley of her breasts. "Remember the Mexican sauce? We are at different levels of love. I've been burned, and wary. The wary stage revolved around several women on a temporary physical basis. I'm beyond being satisfied by a taste. I want it all."

Shrugging into his shirt, he levered himself up before tucking in his shirttail. "I'll be back tomorrow."

Crystal was too emotionally drained to argue, or to stop him from departing. When the door closed behind him, she rolled face forward into the sofa-back cushion. Tears of frustration gathered in the corners of her eyes, threatening to fall.

"Five seconds more and I'd have followed him out of here on my knees," she groaned aloud, clutching the soft pillow and wishing it were harder . . . more masculine.

Scotty and Mac bounced on the sofa, nuzzling her hand and arm. Hugging both of them to her chest, averting her face from their wet tongues, she broke into laughter.

"You rascals. Just because Brett allowed you to wash his face doesn't mean you're going to mop up my tears with your tongues."

There was something consoling about having two affectionate pets wagging their tails with such energy that their whole rear ends shook.

"Come on, boys. We'll take our walk now," she said, rewarding them for raising her spirits. "Get your coats."

Their favorite command sent them scrambling into the kitchen to get their leashes. Crystal had trained them as pups to do this trick when she found herself on several occasions frantically searching for their misplaced leashes. Now they no longer had to cross their back legs and wait at the door when nature called. Again laughter bubbled from Crystal when both dogs ran back to the couch dragging their 'coats.' With great dignity they dropped the contents of their mouths and patiently waited for their mistress to click them onto their collars.

The exercise was a tonic for all of them. The frustration she had felt when Brett had left was briskly eliminated as she jogged along the bike path with Scotty and Mac. Only the silky fabric, sensually moving against her unrestrained breasts, reminded her of what had taken—and not taken—place. A warm euphoria close to happiness settled around her.

"Crystal, you're falling in love," she said to herself out loud.

What other reason could account for her sense of well-being. Like most teenagers, she had been in love with love, and been infatuated with many of the male species. But this was the first time in ages she had been truly fascinated by a man. Brett met all the criteria, all the high standards, other men had fallen sadly short of.

Not only was he tall, dark, and handsome; he had an inner beauty shining from within. Of course, she reasoned, there were a *few* things she wanted to change. She wouldn't place him on a marble pedestal and be disappointed to find feet of clay.

He is terribly conservative, she thought, beginning to list traits she felt were less than admirable. Mentally she pictured him in snug jeans and a worn T-shirt. Somehow the image was fuzzy, not in focus. Surely he isn't impeccably dressed all the time. Then she remembered Brett giving himself a quick once over in the hall mirror before leaving her apartment. Being well dressed was important to him. Breathing deeply from the exertion of running, she chastized herself for feeling the need to change Brett. After all, being conservatively well dressed wasn't a crime.

But then again, she silently argued, he is straitlaced about other things that are important. There was no doubt he didn't approve of her assignment, and he certainly squelched the interview with Annette.

Did he object to her profession as a whole? Or did he object to this one particular assignment? Her running slowed to a brisk stroll as she mulled over the questions. Was it possible she could not reach the high standards he would set? Hadn't he been adamant when he refused to sign the photo releases? Why?

Brett was right, she mused. They had gone too far, too fast. Their physical attraction had bypassed some major curves in the road.

It was futile to become emotionally involved with a man who considered her work demeaning. Hadn't she been trained since early childhood to be independent? To think for herself? Her parents had not wanted her to leave the small town in the Missouri boot heel where she had been raised, but they had understood her need to be on her own. They had encouraged her to stretch her horizons past the confines of being a reporter on the local newspaper. Being independent, self-supporting, and decisive was deeply ingrained.

Momentarily she wondered if Brett was contemplating the changes he would make in her life-style.

"Not my job, man," she muttered resolutely. "That is where I draw the line!"

Chapter Six

Sunday morning Crystal was up, dressed, and had eaten before the telephone rang.

"Hello," she answered with early morning exuberance.

"It's Mike, your boss."

"Okay, boss. Don't chew me out for sending Chad home yesterday," she rattled. "I had other plans."

"Brett?"

"Hmmmm. Not that it is any of my boss's business, but yes."

The confirmation of his suspicions left Mike momentarily silent. Crystal knew he was debating whether or not to interfere in her personal life.

"About the arrangements for today," he began with the same gruff voice he used at work,

"I've told Chad to pick you up at ten. Let him ask for the signatures on the release forms."

"Mike," she protested, "I don't need Chad to do that."

"Take some E.B.S. shots at the baseball field at Parkway North. They're practicing for the state tournament," he continued, discounting her interruption. "The zoo is another possibility. On your way around try the Air Force base. Men in uniform appeal to women."

"Michael . . . I don't want Chad along supervising," Crystal insisted. "Brett volunteered."

"He what?" Mike sputtered. "Let me warn you . . . if you like the man, don't take him along."

"Why?" Crystal retorted, her curiosity provoked.

"He has reasons I'm not at liberty to disclose. Follow my advice and send him home."

The dogs barking at the door frantically signaled the approaching heavy footsteps of a man.

"That's one of them now. I'll talk to you at work."

"Crystal . . ."

Dropping the receiver into place, Crystal quieted the dogs and answered the door.

Scotty and Mac, jumping eight feet off the

floor, welcomed Brett with the enthusiasm Crystal wanted to show herself. Even in those gawky, awkward teenage years, she had been too spunky to be shy. The constriction in her throat was a new experience.

"Down! Down, Scotty," Brett ordered, petting each dog vigorously. With a wink he said huskily, "Not much of a welcome to the returning hero on your part. What's the matter, Crystal? Afraid I'll jump you?"

No, she thought silently, I'm afraid I'll leap on *you*. Oh, for the life of a dog, she bemoaned, hating the unfamiliar shyness that kept her from reacting as spontaneously.

"That's the best offer I've had today," she said cheekily. "Come on in and we'll compare skeletons."

Barely moving out of the doorway, his eyes swept over her powder-blue skirt and matching cashmere sweater, then lingered on her face. Reaching out, he folded her into his arms, hugging her ferociously.

"Mmmm. You feel good, and smell good." Kissing her lightly, he added, "Taste good, too."

Cupping his lower jaw with both hands, she briefly returned the kiss before stepping away.

"Cup of coffee?" she offered, deciding to impart the bad news of his being unable to accompany her with the width of the dinette set between them.

"Thanks. Black, please."

Setting the hot brew on the table, Crystal said, "I have to work today."

"I'm the raw recruit you drafted, remember? Reporting for duty, ma'am, bright and early and bushy-tailed." He smiled as her eyebrow winged upward.

"Contrary to popular belief—yours to be specific, and Mike's to be more general—I am perfectly capable of conducting myself as a professional and completing the task *alone*." She knew he was punching her button, but couldn't keep the haughty words locked behind her teeth.

Brett chuckled at her predictable response. "You'll be glad I'm with you ... later."

She tried but couldn't keep her lips from twitching. "Why not now?" she asked in a sultry, seductive voice.

"You're too eager," he retorted quickly, taking a sip of coffee but impaling her with a level stare.

"Why you conceited ..."

The grin became a chuckle, then deep laughter as Brett tipped the chair back on two back legs. Realizing she had been baited and trapped sharpened her wits.

Elbows on the table, she rested her chin on her palms. "I can't resist your eyes...those broad shoulders...and those oh-so-rounded, perfectly firm buns." She had to cover her mouth to hide the grin when the front legs of his chair slammed down on the floor. There was no way he could know she was quoting the comments written on a survey.

"You're drooling like a teenager over a Burt Reynolds centerfold." His eyes changed from a warm black to polished onyx.

"Men observe women's curves. Why shouldn't I admire your physique?" she heckled.

"That is different," he retorted vehemently.

Crystal's honey-colored eyes twinkled merrily as they assessed his physical attributes in the same manner she had seen men strip the clothing off women. She schooled her face into a lecherous leer and watched the deep scarlet stain creep up his neck.

"You're asking for it!" he growled, stalking around the table.

"Are you going to give it to me?" she asked, running the tip of her tongue over her lower lip.

Brett lifted her off the chair, locking his arms around her neck as she let the laughter bubble out.

"Don't let me see you undressing any other man, or I'll throttle you and smash your camera."

"Smash my camera?" she teased. "Bodily harm and destruction of my most prized possession? I'd better leave you here and take Chad along."

"No way. I don't trust him, either. I'm going," he informed her huskily into her ear.

"Chad is harmless. He wants my job . . . not my body. All talk and no action."

"Given provocation, no man is all talk and no action. Besides," he added, nibbling her earlobe and catching the golden post running through her pierced ear between his teeth, "you aren't aware of how a man feels when you take his picture and talk about sex appeal."

"Mmmmm? How did you feel?"

"Excited." He trailed kisses over her throat when she arched her neck invitingly. "Strong. Virile."

Looping her arms around his waist, Crystal relished his touch. "Made your starched shorts steam, hmmm?"

Brett leaned back and flicked his finger lightly down her straight nose. "Do you always talk in sexual innuendos?" he asked seriously.

"Do you like it?"

Pausing, thinking before replying, he moved

backward against the countertop, taking her with him. "Not if you are this provocative with all men," he answered truthfully. "Are you?"

Crystal rubbed her knuckles across his cheek, loving the sandpaper roughness of a heavy beard closely shaven.

"Do you seduce all women with your eyes and hands?" she asked, smoothing the furrows on his brow.

"You're hedging."

"No," she contradicted. "I'm telling you how you affect women."

"You talk too much. Kiss me . . . properly."

More slowly than a slow-motion film, Crystal rose up and met his lips. Sweet, oh, so sweet, she thought, enticing him to deepen the kiss by parting her lips. Her head spun dizzily when her toes lost contact with the floor.

When the door bell pealed, they both groaned.

"It's Chad," she said softly against his lips, unwilling to leave the sanctuary of his arms.

"Double groan."

The door bell rang again and again.

"Coming," Crystal shouted as she moved in the direction of the door. "For heaven's sake, Chad, keep your britches on."

With a jerk she flung open the door.

"You decided you want my buns after all?"

he asked, swaggering in and unbuckling his belt.

"Triple groan," Crystal blurted in exasperation. "Keep your britches on is a colloquialism ... not an invitation."

"The safety commercial on television advises to 'buckle up and save a life,'" Brett commented icily from the kitchen doorway.

"Are you threatening me?" Chad asked, bristling aggressively.

"Yes."

Glancing at Crystal, it was apparent that Chad did not want to lose face by backing down in front of a woman, but the fear in his eyes revealed he wasn't wild about the prospect of having his face pushed in either. Brett's display of jealousy was unwarranted. How many times did she have to reassure him that Chad was a viper, not a lover?

"Gentlemen?" Crystal queried, interrupting the exchange, "shall we get the work completed first? Then you two can duke it out ... outside."

Going to the front closet, she collected her camera equipment while babbling Mike's suggestions to Chad nonstop. Speed was of the essence if she were to avoid having her furniture smashed to smithereens.

The hostility increased between Brett, who

was driving the car, and Chad who was in the backseat attempting to be funny by making jibes about the driver's cautious handling of the car. His not-so-funny remarks were met with a stony stare from Crystal and the grinding of teeth by Brett.

"What kind of buns appeal to you?" Chad asked, directing the question to Crystal as she climbed out of the car unassisted.

"Hamburger buns," she muttered, glaring at him, wanting to push him back in the car and lock the door.

"Ah, baby, you're not even qualified for the powder-puff work. Good thing I'm around," he retorted smugly. "You carry the equipment and let the old pro take over the picture-taking."

"I'm warning you, Chad... backoff and zip your lips," she hissed, trudging on his dilapidated tennis shoes.

Grimacing, Chad raised his hand, preparing to push her away.

"You'll be picking up litter with your teeth if you touch her," Brett ground out while circling behind the back of the car. "Women and small children your speed?"

"That does it!" Chad replied, backing off several paces. "You play bodyguard." Anger flashed from behind his glass-rimmed eyes. Kicking a can out of the gutter, Chad ambled down the sidewalk, taking his anger out on an inanimate object.

"Fan-tas-tic!" Crystal said sarcastically, stretching the single word out. "I'll have hell to pay Monday over this."

"Don't worry about it," Brett said, swinging the camera case strap over one shoulder, then placing his fingers on her elbow and guiding her toward the baseball field.

"Fine for you to say. You don't share a postage-stamp size office with him."

She knew what the work week would be like. Hadn't she been the victim of Chad's vindictiveness on other occasions? Never anything overt, just annoying rumors buzzing in the press room, or supplies mysteriously missing from her work cabinet. Confronting him had been pointless. He would smile and make a smart remark about career women not making it in business due to lack of organization. Having to back down in front of a masculine third party, and being angry enough to strike her, boded dark clouds on the horizon.

"I'll call Mike to explain what happened," Brett said solicitously, opening the cyclone fence leading into the practice field.

"Don't you dare!" she exclaimed. "You'll make me the laughingstock of the entire magazine."

"But—"

"No *buts,*" she interrupted.

Pulling her around and marching back out of the gate, Brett propelled her toward the car. Seeing the twinkle in his dark eyes, Crystal planted her feet firmly, digging in her heels, and refused to budge.

"What the hell are you doing?" she demanded.

"You said . . . no butts," he replied, grinning.

The pun wasn't lost on Crystal. She knew she should be furious with his domineering manhandling, but her own keen sense of humor wouldn't let her.

"You're infuriating," she said, taking the sting out with a wide smile and a chuckle.

"Just a raw recruit following orders, ma'am," he teased lightly.

"Well, in the future don't take my commands so literaly, private."

Brett's attention was diverted by a man approaching them with COACH lettered on his jacket.

"Hi, coach," Crystal greeted, stepping in front of Brett. "We're from *St. Louis City* magazine. Mind if I take a few pictures of the team?"

The exceptionally tall blond-headed athlete stopped abruptly at the request. When his eyes drifted over Crystal, a slight grin brought a dimple to one cheek.

"Want a picture of the state champs, huh?" he drawled, pride in the team evident.

"Not exactly. I'm doing an article on what attracts women to men, and my boss thought using young athletes was a good idea. Would you mind signing a release form in their behalf?"

"Release form?" he repeated skeptically. "If the parents object, it could be a big hassle for me."

"The parents might not want their sons mooning for a magazine," Brett agreed, playing the devil's advocate."

"Mooning?"

Crystal kicked Brett's shin—unobtrusively, she hoped. The sharp intake of air on impact gave her immediate satisfaction.

"Not mooning," she replied, giving a strangled laugh. "I don't need them naked."

"Perhaps you should be more specific as to what part of their anatomy you would be photographing," Brett suggested, stepping to the side before she could strike again.

"Eyes. Shoulders," she responded, gulping between each word. A prod in her back made the last distasteful part of the assignment hiccup out, "Buns."

"You're kidding," the blond giant gasped. "You're not kidding!" His eyes darted between the grinning man and the woman whose lips were tightly compressed. "No way, lady. They'll string me up as a pervert. Sorry." Turning on his heel, the coach loped across the field toward his waiting team.

"You're a big help," Crystal said, wheeling toward Brett.

"You and Mike didn't plan ahead. I knew they wouldn't allow any type of exploitation."

"Are you accusing me of sexually exploiting young boys?" she gritted out.

"Perhaps exploitation is a bit strong. However, I am aware of what a publishing house can get away with, and what can get them in trouble."

She hated to admit it, but Brett was right. It hadn't been three months since *SLM* had run an article on adults exploiting their children. Mike had flubbed.

"Let's head toward Forest Park," she said, not pursuing the issue any further.

"Great! I heartily approve of taking pictures of zebra eyes, monkey shoulders, and lion buns."

Chuckling, Crystal walked toward the car. On a beautiful spring day like today the zoo would be packed with people buns, too.

Forest Park was one of her favorite places. Her parents had never failed to take her to the zoo as a child, when they were visiting friends in St. Louis. The free animal shows, the Children's Zoo, which held baby animals, Cat Country, where lions and tigers roamed uncontained by iron bars . . . all of it made for a tourist attraction unrivaled in the Midwest.

Pushing through the turnstile at the entrance of the park, Crystal reached into her purse for train fare money and rushed toward the booth selling tickets.

"Hurry up, Brett. We'll miss the train," she shouted back over her shoulder.

"Whoa! We'll ride the train later. Let's walk up and see the bears first."

Catching up with her, Brett took her hand, weaving their fingers together. Flashing him a smile, she hugged his arm against her side.

"Don't let me forget why I'm here," she said, matching his long stride.

People were milling around the waist-high rock barrier surrounding the moat between the languishing bears and their appreciative audience. One polar bear was sitting in the middle of a small pool of water splashing at the surface as water gushed down from a higher point outside of the bear pen.

Taking her camera off Brett's shoulder, Crystal snapped several pictures of the bears and several more of the men in the area.

Brett watched her ask for the necessary signatures with amusement lighting his face. Most of her subjects were politely surprised. None of them refused to sign.

"Which way?" he asked when she returned to his side.

"Over to the Children's Zoo," she said gaily.

Going to the left, they crossed the railroad track, their strides lengthening as they went downhill. "You seem very familiar with the zoo area," Crystal commented.

"Aren't all native St. Louisans?" Brett replied, giving her a boyish grin. "It's a good place to get away."

"What do rich little boys need to escape from?" she teased.

"In my case, a military academy," he replied, his smile fading. "My parents thought the training and self-discipline would quiet down some of my rebellious ways."

"And did it?"

"Just the opposite. It turned teenage rebellion into open warfare. What were you like as a teenager?"

Gawky, gauche, and grumpy, she answered silently. "Well, let's see. I made my debut at the

Veiled Prophet Ball surrounded by swains begging for my hand in marriage. Of course, I had to refuse. It wasn't possible for me to marry before I had taken the Grand Tour, you see."

Brett gave her a firm swat for tweaking his rich nose.

"I detect a Southeast Missouri twang. My guess is you were Prom Queen, head cheerleader, and...champion of the debate squad."

Crystal merrily guffawed at his being so far from the truth. She knew he wouldn't believe her if she told him she hadn't even been invited to the prom, much less been Prom Queen.

"You were right about the twang," she retorted, avoiding any of the other allegations. "I grew up in a little town south of Sikeston."

"And now you're a big-city reporter. I'll bet your folks are proud of you, aren't they?"

"Mother has been known to wave copies of *SLM* in the middle of town," she said, beaming at him. "But think...everytime your folks pick up a phone, they think of you."

"That is a bone of contention I don't care to discuss," he said solemnly. The grim look on his face didn't encourage Crystal to inquire further.

Inside the small building housing the zoo's

baby animals, children ran from cage to cage, poking their fingers between the small wire mesh, trying to touch the small animals. Zoo attendants periodically would remove an animal and let the curious children stroke them. The right-hand side of the building was devoted to a nursery for the chimpanzees and a kitchen for preparing food.

Satisfied that she had seen all of the exotic animals, Crystal strolled out the back door with Brett close behind. A man-made creek wandered around, creating the illusion of a creek surrounded by boulders. Large wooden cutouts of various animals painted in bright colors made the place perfect for taking pictures of children willing to pose.

When Brett stooped to get a drink from the child-size drinking fountain placed in the jaws of a wooden lion, Crystal was there to snap a picture. Following a path that took them into a tunnel, they gazed up and saw fish indigenous to Missouri lazily swimming in a pond overhead whose bottom was made of clear glass.

Climbing a steep flight of stone steps single file, they entered an enclosure for mountain-climbing goats. Small cups of feed and bottles of milk were sold at a stand in one corner. Hungry goats clustered around children holding the food. It was the one place in the zoo where the sign DO NOT FEED THE ANIMALS was noticeably absent.

They watched in amazement as sure-footed goats nimbly clambered up and down the boulders on ledges incredibly narrow. Crystal stepped back to photograph a group of children feeding the animals. When they ran out of bottles, she went to the stand and purchased more.

Turning around, hands full, she held her breath when she saw Brett. Bent double at the waist, he had stooped over to tie his shoe. Pawing the ground a few feet behind him, a small white goat was taking aim. Before she could shout out a warning, the goat had charged, hitting Brett square in the rear end, knocking him flat on the ground, facedown.

"Brett," she screamed, rushing to his side. "Are you hurt?"

Face averted, he groaned loudly. Crystal stepped over his prone body and began running her hands across his shoulders. A group of children were beginning to gather around them, forming a small huddle.

"Oh, Brett," she whimpered, not knowing what to do. One hand covered his face as his shoulders began to shake. *He's crying.* She could hear strangled, muffled sounds coming from his chest. Kneeling down in the dirt, she felt her sheer nylons pop a run. It didn't matter. Nothing mattered to her other than finding someone to give medical assistance.

Pulling his hand away to check for blood, she froze. Instead of a jagged cut oozing blood, she saw a wide, toothy grin.

"Going to kiss it well?" Brett asked in a whisper.

"You fraud!" Crystal shouted, jumping to her feet. Another run popped.

Jackknifing up, he smiled at the children. In a conspiratorial voice he said to them, "Isn't that the way it's done by the clowns in the circus?"

Joyously they giggled and began clapping their hands.

"Do it again," one youngster shouted.

Brushing the dirt and sawdust from his trousers and shirt, he joined in their laughter. Only one person wasn't amused. The one with the shredded nylons.

"Are you really a clown, mister?" a cute little girl with blond banana curls asked.

"He certainly is," Crystal replied, heading toward the gate that led out of the enclosure. Her lips began to tilt upward.

No one had played a trick on her like that in

years. Gus, her brother, was a great one for "playing dead" at the slightest injury. She remembered once, when they had been walking a log across Little River, Gus had pointed below to the crawdads.

"Don't let the crocodiles get you," he teased. "They'll pinch you and pinch you until lightning strikes."

A few minutes later, crawdad dangling from his finger, he ran lickity-split past her on the path leading to their house.

"It got me!" he screamed over and over.

Immediately she had raised her head and begun to pray for rain clouds. The smile on her face widened at the memory.

Laughter passed through her lips as she relived seeing Brett being butted to the ground. Leaning against the gate, she laughed harder and harder. She had been so scared, and that lummox had been faking!

The remainder of the afternoon was spent in lighthearted, gay abandon. Brett bought hot dogs and popcorn at the main concession stand. He poked the wiener into her mouth, piece by piece, then fed the roll and the popcorn to the ducks in the pond nearby.

In each house he would drop tidbits of knowledge about the animals. Some of the information he gathered from reading the small plaques beside each enclosure, and the remainder he made up. By the time they left each house, Crystal was giggling hysterically.

If, as Brett had mentioned, she saw everything in black and white, this would be classified as an all-white, shining, glorious day.

Chapter Seven

Days and nights flew by, unclocked by Greenwich time. Spring in St. Louis passed with its usual briefness, leading into the sweltering, humid heat of summer. The city came alive, not only with the hustle and bustle of workers going to and from work, but also by the invasion of tourists. License plates could be seen from any state in the nation on the Gateway to the West's parking lot, which bordered the waterfront.

The entire waterfront area on the banks of the mighty Mississippi thronged with crowds. The two passenger cars carrying visitors to the top of the Arch were in constant use. Few suburbanites realized the Arch and Western Movement Museum were the third most visited national monuments in the United States, but the inner-city workers knew.

The excitement in the air affected everyone, Crystal included. There were times when she wondered if she had been only half alive before Brett had stormed into her apartment. The part of her heart that had been held in a comatose state was gradually filling with love.

On the days when she didn't see Brett, he called. Her world seemed to be pivoting on an axis named Brett Masterson. He made her feel beautiful, almost glamorous.

The money she had hoarded in a savings account was dwindling at the same pace her wardrobe was increasing. Polyester pantsuits were gradually shifted to the rear of her closet and replaced with softer, more feminine, two-piece skirted suits made of natural fibres.

The sterility of her apartment had changed also. Green gifts from Brett hung from the ceiling in every room. Houseplants lined the fireplace and sat on each tabletop. The rooms were alive with multicolored foliage.

Chad was the minor blight in her life. Since the confrontation between him and Brett, he no longer pretended to be part of a working team. His thin upper lip was permanently locked into the snarl position. When an opportunity arose to make a disparaging remark, he jumped on it with both flat feet. Working together in the same cramped office was passing difficult, and becoming impossible.

Hellatious would be the most apt description, Crystal thought as she searched for the box of pencils in the tall gray supply cabinet. Glancing over her shoulder, she saw several lying on the desk abutting hers.

Returning to her desk empty-handed, Crystal considered snatching one and damn the consequences. Momentarily she pictured the two of them playing tug-of-war with the yellow pencil being the prize.

"Daydreaming about lover boy?" Chad asked snidely. "*SLM* should put you on piece work. Your production rate wouldn't earn you enough to have your hair done." Brett and her hair, although not necessarily in that order, were the two favorite topics of the week.

"I'd like a pencil, please," Crystal said, unwilling to be baited.

"You've ground up your share. That new electric pencil sharpener ate them while you were daydreaming." Chad laughed hollowly at what he thought was funny.

Reaching into her purse, Crystal began pulling out odds and ends, piling them on her desk, as she searched the bottom for a writing instrument.

"They say a woman's mind is like the contents of her purse," he jabbed, watching the pile spread.

Silently counting to ten, she ignored the remark. Smiling as her fingertips touched a ballpoint pen, she felt as though she were the winner in a scavenger party.

Giving Chad a defiant glare and nonchalantly raking the pile back in her purse, Crystal sent the message over the desktop that she couldn't care less about his theories on the organized woman.

"How's the E.B.S. story coming along?" he asked, tossing a pencil stub with the eraser gnawed off over to her desk.

"Great." A monosyllabic reply snapped from between a rigidly held jaw.

Bending her head, she reread the written copy that would accompany the pictures. Crystal chuckled to herself. Since women fluctuated between what masculine features consistently drew their attention, she had decided to use a paper-doll theme. Using an array of physiques clothed with everything from tailored suits to jogging shorts, the subscriber could mix and match according to her own tastes. The final combination would be the reader's own personal version of the 'ideal man.'

Gathering the layouts of the pictures and the

written text, she left the hostile atmosphere in their office and briskly strode to the door labeled EDITOR. Rapping twice, she entered when Mike's secretary nodded and gestured for her to go on in.

"I'm working on the final draft of the E.B.S. story. Want to see how it's coming along?"

"You appear to be on top of the world, old buddy," Mike replied, taking the stack of papers from her hands. "Another new outfit?" he asked, taking in the creamy beige silk-blend suit and ruffled coordinated blouse in one all-encompassing sweep.

"I'm going out after work with Brett," she replied as she casually draped herself on the corner of his desk.

"Hot date, huh?"

"Anything is within the realm of possibility," she quipped coyly, dodging the question.

Mike would probably be shocked if he knew how platonically Brett was treating her. They had reverted back to the hand-holding stage. Occasionally she had managed to slip past his iron-clad defenses and have him breathing heavily between mind-drugging kisses, but that was the exception, not the rule.

"He's like bubble gum...you're not talking while the flavor lasts?" he teased unmercifully.

Crystal grinned. "*You* have the bubble-gum personality . . . filled with hot air and popping off all the time."

"Smart mouth," he retorted, chuckling at the appropriate analogy. "Down to business." With keen perception he began reading the context and looking at the collage of pictures.

Holding her breath, waiting for the curt nod of approval, Crystal anxiously awaited his decision. When he began flipping back through the pages, she knew he wasn't satisfied.

"You definitely aren't a 'buns' woman, are you?" Mike asked as he shuffled through the photographs.

Crystal couldn't deny the obvious. Proportionately the eye and shoulder shots outnumbered the other pictures five to one. She could make excuses for the deficiency, but didn't. "No," she replied succinctly without explanation.

"That's precisely why Chad does better newspaper work than you. When he is given a three-part assignment he meticulously reports on each part. However, we both know Chad has other problems."

Too many to list and still make it home for Thanksgiving turkey, Crystal silently, unprofessionally thought. Mike was opening the conversation up for criticism of her officemate, but she resisted telling him exactly how difficult Chad made her life.

"Good," Mike praised, apparently realizing she was biting her tongue. "You're handling the work space situation admirably. On the other hand, you tend to be biased in your reporting. A reporter has to be open to all facets of a subject. Objectivity, without emotionalism, is the key. While Chad may be a rat in his professional relationships, he does manage to represent the most obscure viewpoints of an issue comprehensively."

Listening carefully, Crystal absorbed the constructive criticism. Mike knew his business. One of the reasons she was no longer relegated to the gourmet section of the magazine was because she heeded his sage advice. Optimistically she hoped this pep talk would advance her another step if she followed the guidelines he was setting forth.

Mike reared back in his chair to see the impact of his words. "Thanks for sugar-coating the pill. I'll take your suggestion and rework the story."

By the end of the workday she had outlined where, how, and when she would obtain additional shots. It would alter her plans for the evening with Brett, but that's the way the cookie crumbled. Completing the article before the deadline was first on her list of priorities. He would understand.

Climbing into his awaiting car, she flashed him a smile and began telling him about her day. As usual, she left out the part about her running feud with Chad. For some reason unknown to Crystal, she only revealed the highlights of her job to Brett. "You don't mind the change in plans, do you?"

"Not if you don't. I had something more romantic in mind, but..." His voice trailed off, leaving the sentence dangling.

"We can be romantic after we drive out to Lake Charles. Hot as it is today, there should be scads of people waterskiing and swimming. I need muscular buns and shoulders."

"You should let Chad complete that part of the assignment," Brett replied coolly, turning onto Highway 70.

"It's my assignment. I don't have any choice."

"Bat those beautiful eyes at your boss and tell him you feel uncomfortable with this portion of the work."

The mood she was in after putting up with Chad and being criticized by Mike was not conducive to accepting the suggestion lightly. Brett didn't know it, but she was spoiling for a fight.

Something to use as a safety valve to keep her from ripping Chad limb from limb.

"Does Annette use feminine wiles to get out of work she doesn't want to do?" The calmly asked question hid the anger just below the surface.

Brett laughed. "You don't have to be jealous of Annette, sweetheart. She's happily married with two kids. Remember?"

"I'm not jealous," she truthfully retorted. "I'm illustrating a point. What choice have you given Annette regarding the care of her children? None!"

"The company has arranged alternative options that are available, free of charge, to all employees."

"Such as?" Crystal questioned.

"The Latch-Key Program. Children too old for a baby-sitter or nursery school are called by a local agency shortly after they arrive home from school.

"What happens when the child doesn't answer the phone?"

"The agency calls a nearby neighbor, or if that fails, notifies the parent, and they jointly decide what the next step should be."

"You haven't removed the worry or the guilt feelings a working mother has. I've interviewed women who complain of stomach cramps and nausea from the stress of knowing their children are on their own. You talk about the expense? Shoplifting is rampant because of unsupervised kids."

"Aren't you generalizing, *again*? You are equating latch-key children and thieves," he said, snorting at the fallacy in her argument.

"Wrong. The telephone company is one small step. When *all* the utility companies and the nation's largest employer, the government, offer on-site day-care facilities, then you'll see a change."

"The biggest change will be in the cost of living. If you pay higher bills and higher taxes, the cost of private day-care is nominal."

"What would you prefer for your own children?" she questioned, knowing the protests of executives changed when it came to their own children.

Brett laughed. "Don't you think we should discuss rings and a honeymoon before we get to where we're going to put our children?"

"I wasn't hinting," she fumed. "Answer the question."

"I'd prefer to have you at home," he replied blandly, refusing to let her off the hook.

Crystal knew she was being pulled into water muddier than the Mississippi. How had he managed to direct the conversation from a societal need to marriage and children? He always seemed able to sway the direction of their discussions to hearth and home. Once again she would have to pull him from the horse-and-buggy age into the twentieth century.

"Isn't that concept rather old-fashioned? Women have earned a place in the work force. I've told you once, but I'll refresh your memory: I love my job."

"I also recall your saying you want to move on to better assignments," he answered. "Being a wife falls into that category."

"Cleaning the house and changing diapers is not my idea of climbing the ladder of success," she stated unequivocally, shaking her head.

"I'm a great boss," Brett said, his grin showing he would also enjoy the intimacies of marriage. "I'll offer fantastic fringe benefits. You'll love your work."

Audibly groaning, Crystal shook her head again, folding her arms across her chest. "Why is it women are the ones expected to make all the changes?" Seeing his face wreathed in smiles, she decided to wipe the grin right off his face. "You could do with a few minor adjustments yourself."

"Care to cite a few examples?"

"Wing-tipped shoes! Starched underwear!" she flung out.

Crystal knew she was being petty, but she had been on the fuzzy end of the lollipop all day, and antagonizing Brett was, for the moment, justifiable.

They had not reached Lambert Airport when Brett took the Brown Road turnoff, crossed over the viaduct, and signaled for a left-hand turn at the stop light.

"Aren't you going to take me out to Lake Charles?" Crystal demanded angrily.

The light changed. Checking his rearview mirror, which seemed to be demanding all of his attention, he eased into the flow of traffic going back into St. Louis.

"I don't know who stepped on your tail today, but I have absolutely no intention of letting you vent your spleen on me." His clenched jaw and compressed lips should have cued Crystal to back off, but unspent anger thrust her rapier tongue forward again.

"This journey wouldn't be necessary if a certain uptight, stiff-necked stick-in-the-mud would sign a release form."

His hands, clasping the steering wheel, turned knuckle white. "I've had the dubious honor of having my photograph in the scandal tabloids," he replied, his voice colder than the Arctic wind.

Crystal laughed harshly. "What happened?

Did a contingent of socialites swoon at your feet, making pests of themselves?''

"Quite the opposite." Brett paused. "One very near and very dear died as a result of yellow journalism."

The car accelerated rapidly. The speedometer she had watched jerked to the right. The powerful Cadillac surged into the passing lane, leaving behind the cars obeying the speed limit.

Staring out of the passenger window, Crystal knew she had stepped in a hornet's nest. Should she apologize? Ask questions? Shut up? She opted not to antagonize him further. Amber eyes searched his stony face, seeking a clue to the meaning of his curt words. His left hand rose, rubbed his forehead, then clamped back onto the wheel.

"I'll drive, if you're getting a headache," she offered softly, extending a verbal olive branch of peace. "I have some aspirin, if they would help."

"No, thanks," he said, rejecting them. "I don't take pills."

The drive back to the city was swift and silent. After the initial burst of speed, the car had slowed down within the boundaries of the law. Brett refused to take his eyes from the highway. Lines of strain made a deep crease beside his straight nose. The self-control he had displayed previously was nominal compared to the control he had to exercise to keep his emotions bottled inside of him now.

Analyzing his statement held no answers for Crystal. *Someone near and dear.* A relative? Friend? Man? Woman? Who had died as a result of seeing his photograph? The five questions drummed into the head of every journalist buzzed forward: who, what, when, where, and why.

As she took a short breath, the first question formed on her lips. She bit it back. The pain etched on his features made her curiosity seem morbid. Whatever had happened obviously had made a wound healed without benefit of antiseptic. Underneath the scar tissue was a raw, festering infection. Probing would be informative but callous.

The anger she had felt building up all day toppled over. She had been a shrew from the moment she had put her foot into the car. Recklessly she had used him as a whipping post. Now she was paying the price.

What an insensitive bitch I am, she lambasted herself. *Shallow. Unfeeling.* By the time they pulled into the parking lot, she had lengthened the list tenfold.

At her door, key in hand, dogs yipping in the background, she debated whether or not he would accept an invitation to come in. He was miserable; she was miserable. She ached with the need to gather him into her arms and comfort him.

"Won't you come in and talk about it?" she asked, barely above a whisper.

"I can't." His dark eyes seemed glued to the tips of his shoes.

"Please, Brett," she coaxed, not wanting him to leave.

A white-hot flame flared in his eyes as they swept over her hungrily, but the pain remained scored into his skin. "Can I stay...permanently?" he asked as his fingers softly closed over her upper arms.

"Brett...?"

The pressure of his hands increased momentarily. The indecision in her voice was quickly decoded. Lifting his shoulders, dropping his hands limply, he accepted the decision. Sketching a brief military salute, he returned to his car without a backward glance.

Braced against the door, she watched the car smoothly pull away from the curb and depart. The humidity, or was it the cold sweat of fear, dampened her skin. The trees were stock-still. For a moment she felt as though the earth had stopped revolving. Nothing appeared to move.

One tear formed, clung to the dark tips of

her eyelashes, then spilled onto her cheek. The magic had gone ... disappeared inside the car whose brake lights flashed at the corner stop sign.

A picture caused a death? The thought hounded Crystal while she spread peanut butter over a stale piece of bread. The expression on his face as he had said the words haunted her as she walked the terriers around the condo complex. What woman or man would kill themselves, commit suicide, to get away from Brett? Had the picture been in a magazine ... a newspaper? Yellow journalism could be found in either one. Pulling a bright coral nightgown over her head, she cursed her lack of information. There was more than one side to this story. Running an emery board across the tip of a jagged nail she had bitten off, Crystal feared she would never know the solution to the mystery unless ...

Picking up the phone, she dialed Mike's number. He would know the answers.

"Hi, Mike ... your old buddy, Crystal, here," she said, identifying herself and the status of the conversation.

"No. I won't allow a rematch before next Saturday, if that's what you called for. How did the picture-taking turn out?"

Crystal groaned. With the problems confronting her, she had completely forgotten about why they had been going out to Lake Charles.

"Brett and I had an argument, and he brought me home."

"You took Brett with you? Didn't I warn you earlier not to take him along? Why he is even interested in you is beyond my comprehension."

"Thanks a lot, boss. I knew I wasn't a Bo Derek, but I didn't picture myself as the Wicked Witch of the West, either."

"What you look like isn't the problem."

"Then what is the problem?"

Mike paused, loudly clearing his throat. "I'm tempted not to answer," he started thoughtfully, "but you ought to know."

After a few moments of silence Crystal prodded, "Well?"

"It's really none of my business," he replied, stalling for time.

Crystal heard Mike place his hand over the receiver. From the muffled tones it sounded as though he were arguing with Jane. Crystal couldn't decipher anything other than a distorted no. This word was spoken as he removed his hand.

"Still there?"

"Yes."

"Jane insists I tell you the whole story, but I don't think it is my story to tell. The whole mess was in the December papers about ten years ago. You're a reporter . . . ferret it out for yourself."

"Thanks, Mike," she said gratefully.

"Don't thank me. I woudn't have told you — didn't tell you, should anyone ask." In other words, don't reveal your source was what she read between the edited lines.

"Mind if I come in at noon tomorrow? I thought I'd check out some buns at the library."

"The library doesn't check out buns, only books," he quipped, knowing full well she would be in the old newspaper section.

Chuckling, Crystal retorted, "Maybe a bit of both, in my case."

"Make certain you at least look for E.B.S. . . . you are on company time," he said mockingly.

"Will do. And Mike . . . thanks again."

"Nothing to thank me for," he replied gruffly, hiding a golden heart behind his gruff exterior.

Halfheartedly the next morning Crystal snapped pictures and had release forms signed by men passing by the stone steps in front of the city library. She was anxiously watching the door for the stooped, elderly gentleman who for years had unlocked the doors. Jamming her camera into the case, she took the steps two at a time when she saw his snowy white head bending over the lock.

"Morning, Sam," she called cordially, hurrying toward the newspaper department. The odor of cleaning fluids and old books assaulted her nostrils as she passed by the checkout desk.

From previous research she knew exactly where to go, and within minutes the microfiche she needed was on the viewing machine. The first sections of the paper were devoid of his name. As she twisted the overhead knob, a black-and-white picture on the society page ended the hunt.

A young Brett Masterson in a close embrace with a tall blond bombshell covered an eighth of the page. Eyes closed, he must not have been aware of the photographer. The gossipy caption below made amber eyes widen. It read: *Wealthy renowned bachelor Brett Masterson welcomes starlet Liz Joyce to Washington. Where is Sally Wilson? Admiring the HUGE engagement ring AT HOME. Once a rake, always a rake, eh, Brett?*

God, how embarrassing it must have been to be seen clutching a woman and have it splashed in the papers for his fiancée to see. How could he explain it to...what's her name...Sally Wilson? Crystal mused.

"Very ambiguously," she said out loud.

Surely his fiancée would have listened. There was, most likely, a plausible reason for the clinch. Brett was no dummy. He probably contacted Sally post haste.

Turning the knob to the next day of publication, Crystal audibly gasped when she read the bold printed headlines. HEIRESS COMMITS SUICIDE. A picture of Sally Wilson was side-by-side with a snapped photo of Brett boarding an airplane angrily shaking his fist.

"Oh, my God," Crystal murmured. "How awful for Brett."

Slowly she began reading the long account of the details. The article was factual, devoid of innuendos. Sally Wilson had been a victim of an overdose of sleeping pills. A suicide note had been left, but it was to be opened by her fiancé, Mr. Brett Masterson, and no one else. The remainder of the news article gave Sally Wilson's elite standing in the local community.

The mystery was unraveling like a string from a ball of twine. The evidence was damning, but despite the facts cited, Crystal was confident Brett had a reasonable explanation. Hadn't she found him to be trustworthy and honorable? It was ironical that he would be considered a rake, when presently he was such a conservative. Had the suicide note been the impetus that had changed his life-style?

Crystal jarred the switch into the off position. From what she knew of Brett, and what she had read, none of it made any sense. It was like reading about twins separated at birth.

Leaving the library, she felt certain she had come up with more questions than answers. All the way back to *SLM* she tried to solve the riddle, unsuccessfully.

Head down, deep in thought, fingers sliding up and down the leather strap of the camera case, she didn't see Chad until he purposely bumped into her.

"It's about time you came to work. We've been ordered"—his head jerked upward—"to work on your E.B.S. article." Tapping his camera case, Chad gave an unpleasant chuckle. "I'm to submit pictures also."

Crystal couldn't have cared less. The assignment was not uppermost in her thoughts. Besides, his tendency to cross over the line of propriety into vulgarity would be edited out by Mike.

"See the man by the elevator? What do you think?" Chad asked, removing his camera and setting the lens.

A tall, dark-haired man stood with his back to Chad and Crystal. He stood in a relaxed pose, suit jacket hooked by one finger hung over his shoulder, one leg bent forward, his well-fitted pants cupped under his bottom, showing a mere trace of underpants. Definitely sexy, Crystal agreed, smiling for the first time all day. He looked like... But it couldn't be Brett; he was at work.

Restraining Chad by gripping his forearm, she raised her camera, snapping several pictures in rapid sequence. As the man shifted his weight to his other foot, the cut of his trouser pulled more snugly across his muscular buttocks. The man turned. Crystal pressed her finger and simultaneously knew she couldn't use the pictures. Brett's handsome face was in the viewfinder, scowling.

Lowering her camera, she stood statuelike. She hoped Brett had come to see her, but feared Mike was the reason for his unexpected visit.

Other pictures flashed in her mind: Brett clasping a starlet; Sally Wilson smiling in the portrait picture; Brett boarding a plane. Feeling Brett willing her to speak she blinked to erase the mental pictures.

"Hello, Brett," she greeted him softly. "What brings you to *SLM*?"

"You," he answered pleasantly. "I left rather abruptly yesterday, and I felt I owed you an explanation. Off the record," he added. "Can I take you somewhere for an early lunch?"

"Do you trust me not to blab your confidences?'' Crystal asked, raising her eyes upward in her search for trust.

"I have to. You won't use the pictures you've taken, and you won't print the story I'm about to tell.'' His hand reached to cup the back of her neck.

An electrical charge tingled from one nerve center to another. "I won't violate that trust.'' The words were a personal oath. One to guard, not to be broken.

Chad, who had remained by the entrance of the building, called snidely, "Aren't you planning on working today either?''

"You go ahead, Chad,'' she replied, not removing her gaze from Brett's face.

Intuitively Crystal knew solving the mystery was more important than a portfolio of pictures. Brett's lips, sensuously brushing over her forehead, confirmed the intuition.

Chapter Eight

The silence between them was strung tightly as
they walked the few blocks between the office
building and the high-rise apartment Brett lived
in. Crystal wanted to question Brett about the
pictures. Holding a tight rein on her impetuos-
ity and biting the tip of her tongue, she quieted
her inborn curiosity. This was his personal life,
a tragedy that had deeply affected him. Jangling
keys and the hum of the rising elevator were
the only sounds between them.

Brett previously had told her where he lived,
but had never invited her into his home. The
private nature of their conversation necessi-
tated being alone without the distractions of
other people. They needed privacy to clear the
air of any and all misconceptions.

As the metal door drew back Brett smiled
cautiously and led her to one of the four hall-

way doors. Ushered in, Crystal immediately felt at home. The traditional style of his furniture reminded her of her own. Her honey-toned eyes noted the attractive blending of blues, beiges, and browns in the attractively grouped furnishings.

"Your home is lovely," she commented sincerely, walking gracefully toward the sofa.

"I'm glad you like it," Brett replied while hanging his suit jacket in the front closet before joining Crystal. "White wine?"

Crystal nodded. Anything more alcoholic would have her head spinning in space. A peanut-butter sandwich last night and skipping breakfast were not conducive to imbibing. His nearness in the elevator, with the musky clean fragrance of aftershave filling her senses as the floor rose beneath her feet, had spiraled her higher than the silent cables lifting the elevator.

Tasting the white, slightly fruity wine, she rolled it over her taste buds, savoring the flavor. Swallowing, she said quietly, "I went to the library today."

Sitting forward on the edge of the sofa, legs apart, glass held loosely between long fingers, Brett questioningly pierced her with dark, glowing eyes.

"Now I know two things: One, you know the bare facts of a distorted story; two, you cared enough to find out about my past." Setting his wine down on the low table, he turned toward Crystal. "It's a gruesome story. Half truth and half speculation on the part of the newspapers."

"You don't *have* to tell me," Crystal injected.

Head resting on the pillowed back rest, Brett gazed at the ceiling as though searching for the past and a way to disclose it with a minimal amount of pain.

"The past is part of me. The main reason I've skirted telling you about it is . . ." Momentarily his eyes closed. "Part of it could badly injure two people I care about."

Opening his eyes, tilting his head toward her, he began in a slow, hushed voice. "The Wilson family and my family have always been close. Sally and I grew up together. As teenagers we both knew what our respective parents expected from us: marriage. I rebelled for a few years and dated the exact opposite of the kind of girls you would take home to Momma. My family tolerated the rebellion, thinking I'd come to heel eventually. And, to their way of thinking, I did." Brett swallowed.

Crystal watched his lids squeeze tight. Instinctively she knew discussing the death of his fiancée was horrendously painful.

"Sally suggested we become engaged to keep our families from breathing down our necks. I went along with it." Brett laughed harshly. "Sally laughingly called it an 'open engagement,' leading nowhere. What I didn't realize at the time was while I was out sowing my wild oats, Sally had become involved with a bum."

Brett leaned forward, picking up his wineglass and taking a quick sip. "*Bum* implies unemployed." Shaking his head, he put the glass down. "That is an inaccurate term. He worked diligently ... he was a drug pusher.

"I suspected the hyper energy and the deep depression could be drug-related, but when I confronted Sally, she shrugged and told me to mind my own business. If her folks knew, they kept it quiet." A wry smile crossed his lips as he cast Crystal a head-to-foot look.

"Funny how you grow up with someone and never know them; and meet a person in the park and feel you've known them forever."

Crystal nodded, comprehending and agreeing. Watching Brett get off the sofa and pace to the window, she also knew the worst part was yet to come.

"My picture in the gossip column didn't influence Sally one way or another. She overdosed because her lover deserted her. She blamed our phony engagement and parental pressure. The note vindicated me, but rambled on and on, abusing the Wilsons." Brett laughed harshly. "The bizarre thing is, it wasn't a suicide note. It was a letter breaking the engagement. She'd planned to find her lover and live with him."

"What did you do with the letter?" Crystal inquired softly.

"Tore it into a million pieces and burned it. I couldn't let her parents suffer from the guilt it would have caused. Sally was probably drugged out of her mind when she wrote it."

Fingering the nubby fabric covering the sofa cushion, Crystal tried to assimilate and make sense out of what she had heard.

It was senseless. Two young people had been maneuvered into a loveless engagement that had resulted in the death of one and the radical change of the other. Or had there been a radical change? Wasn't the safety and security she felt with Brett the same quality Sally must have known? She had camouflaged a lover, drugs, and who knows what else, by using Brett as a shield. Crystal admired the courage it had taken to shred the note that would have exonerated him.

Patting the seat, she silently gestured for him to come closer. Telling the story had taken a toll on both of them. Before he took her hands and sat down, his eyes glittered over her face.

"I'm not interested in pity."

What she was feeling was a long way from pity. Budding love, admiration, respect—all of these, but not pity.

"Are you disgusted with me for being so spineless as to have been pushed into a phony engagement?"

The fleshy part of her thumbs were being stroked in a circular motion, causing her finger-tips to curl around his hands. The magnetism of his eyes drew her breath from her lungs.

"The exact opposite of disgust," she mur-mured when his grip on her thumbs tightened, demanding a response.

Taking her hands, he placed them on his vest. With infinite care his arms surrounded her slender body and lifted her onto his lap. Crystal nestled against his chest, listening to the calm, rhythmic thudding of his heartbeat. Lightly his hands roamed over her back. A small shudder shook his strong frame as he drew a deep breath and expelled it.

"My shoulders feel as though a ton of weight had been lifted from them." He chuckled. "Ironic, isn't it? I rattled the skeleton in my closet . . . to a snoopy reporter?"

Kissing his throat sweetly, Crystal murmured between light pecks, "You can trust me."

For long moments Brett silently held her, cherishing the trust they were sharing. "It's been ages since I trusted anyone," he confided. A whisper of breath kissed the loose tendrils of hair by her temple. "It feels good. You feel good."

The same emotion of goodness, rightness, swept through Crystal. As he extracted the long hairpins binding her hair at the nape of her neck, he massaged her scalp with the other hand. A flicker of desire, like a small candle, was lit. The wavering flame highlighted a new discovery. She could quickly douse the desire, but she could not extinguish the love burning brightly in her soul.

Her darkened eyelashes lowered when she admitted the truth to herself. Her quest for information was not to satisfy the portion of her heart labeled *reporter*. All along she had believed in his honor and strength of character. Hadn't she repeatedly questioned the news articles, never doubting his basic integrity? She had been shocked at the content, but had immediately doubted the authenticity.

A new, hot fever rushed through her veins when Brett unwound the long tangled mass of hair and buried his face in its soft, silky texture.

The stimulated nerve endings of her scalp seemed to extend to the blunt tips of each hair when he pulled them to his lips. Crystal almost felt the warm moistness clinging to the strands of hair.

"You're so lovely. I don't know which part I want to touch most," he said huskily. "Each hair has a life of its own." Fingers spread, small strands clinging to his flesh, then cascading down like a dark waterfall.

"Men had the right idea in the Dark Ages, when they made their woman cover their hair."

"A wimple? Today? In the Eighties? Women wouldn't allow the restriction," she teased lightly.

"I wouldn't ask it anyway. I love seeing it loose." As he tilted her head back, his luminous eyes washed over her face. "Wimples don't cover your most attractive feature anyway."

"My freckles?" she questioned, remembering his father's saying.

"Mmmmm. Gold dust. Tiny beauty marks."

"Beauty marks are black," she softly corrected.

"Maybe yours are golden because they sprinkle across and shelter hidden beauty."

Crystal smiled. "If that's the case, I wasted a lot of money on freckle-fading ointment."

Lightly his lips ran from her high cheek-bones, over the bridge of her nose, and back again. His closed lips were tilted upward in a partial smile as her fingertips moved over his face in a similar path. The side of her thumb traced his thin upper lip and the fuller, more sensual lower lip.

"Kiss me, love. Cauterize the wounds of the past with the purity of your fire," he begged, lowering his head and capturing her lips.

The fire of passion, denied during the past weeks, burst. Brett had made her feel beautiful... treasured... unlike any woman he had ever held.

Opening her lips, she simultaneously opened her heart for him to explore. Perhaps he could reach the tightly curled part deep inside hiding the insecure, less-than-beautiful teenager. The tip of his tongue entered slowly, seeking her own. His swirled, darted back, then swirled again. Copying the intimacy, Crystal moaned as each thrust pulled them closer and closer. A myriad of flaming bright colors burst behind her closed lids. Orange. Red. Yellow. Blue. Nature's pure colors. As she arched toward him, demanding to be held in love's closest embrace, her chest felt as though the colors had scorched her skin.

I want him, Crystal thought mindlessly, madly. *I want him to stoke the fires until they consume both of us.*

When she began tugging at his tie, Brett's arm muscles contracted, restricting her from the space needed to remove the clothing barrier between them.

Ending the soul-searing kiss, he covered her agitated hands. "Crystal, please." His fingers rebuttoned the one opening, the single button at his collar she had managed to undo.

"I want to touch you."

His strong arms crushed her against his hard chest. He buried his dark, passionate face inside the curve between her shoulder and neck.

"I can't be strong this time; I want you so badly my teeth ache. I die a thousand deaths when we kiss and part."

"Don't stop this time. Love me. Come inside and be part of me."

"I want to . . . God knows, I want to." His lips nipped at the tender softness of her throat, but Crystal could feel he still had control over his ardor.

What could she do to snap that control? Frustration and sexual tension divided them. She had pleaded with him to complete their lovemaking. What more could a woman do? One word flashed in her brain . . . *commitment.* He didn't want their lovemaking to be a mere physical release. He wanted more than temporary easing of the fire burning in his loins.

Crystal tried to string her thoughts together. She wanted him. Would words be enough?

"I want you to love me."

They weren't enough. He began withdrawing, retreating behind a wall of steel.

"I love you," Crystal blurted out, somewhat surprised by her own words.

Hesitantly Brett raised his head, almost as though he thought he had heard her, but couldn't believe his ears.

"Say it again," he commanded. His dark eyes boring into the sweet honey color of hers, he repeated, "Say it again . . . mean it."

A radiant smile lit her face. "I love you, Brett Masterson, and I have never said those words to any man."

In one swift motion Brett stood, held her up in his arms, and strode toward the back of the apartment.

She hadn't lied, she silently rationalized. She did love Brett. Maybe, just maybe, he would be able to destroy once and for all the doubts she felt about herself. Closing her eyes, she anticipated the rapture of being loved by Brett. At this moment he could have been carrying her to an open elevator shaft and she wouldn't have noticed.

Feet touching the plush carpet, she found herself unable to support her own weight and swayed against Brett's strength. He held her closely, allowing her to know the full force of the passionate response she had induced.

The restrictive clothing hampered the touch of skin to skin. Brett seemed to be waiting. For what? her mind questioned. Hadn't she bound herself closely enough by the three most important words in any lover's vocabulary? The question strengthened her legs and gave purpose to her fingers.

Capturing the sun smoldering in his eyes, Crystal began undressing him. The vest, shirt, and pants were sensually, not hastily, removed. Nudging him back on the bed, she bent down to take off his shoes and socks. The sensitive tip of each toe was caressed. Never breaking contact, she stroked from ankle to muscular calf to upper thigh. Sliding her hands under the elasticized waistband, she took off the last barrier of clothing covering him.

"Magnificent," she praised, sweeping her eyes from the crown of his head downward, pausing briefly at the evidence of his arousal, then continuing on to the muscular length of his legs.

He started to rise, reaching toward her. Crystal knew he wanted to perform the same disrobing services for her, but stopped his upward movement by stepping back. She wanted to uncover herself, layer by layer, to further his pleasure.

Brett understood. The pillow on the other side of the king-size bed was pulled from beneath the bedspread and piled on top of the other one. Fingers laced together as if to be kept from reaching out were locked behind his head.

One by one, with no great speed, Crystal slowly unbuttoned her tailored blouse. The V in front deepened to her waist before she shrugged out of it. Only a flesh-colored lacy bra covered her torso. Bending her arms behind her back, she released the three hooks she found there.

A sharp intake of breath was Brett's immediate reaction to watching the wisp of lingerie fall to the floor. The muscles of his biceps visibly bulged, but his hands remained behind his head.

"You're torturing a fallen warrior," he accused hoarsely.

Crystal smiled. The unzipping of her skirt seemed louder than a bodice being ripped off. She bent forward, and the thin golden chain and attached ivory unicorn swayed in harmony with the fullness of her breasts as she shed her half slip and panties.

The fire behind his dark eyes leaped over the tender hidden flesh. "Come ... be my woman ..." he invited, unlocking his fingers and reaching up toward her.

"With the greatest of pleasure, milord," she whispered.

And it was the greatest of pleasures. She had set the pace, and Brett followed her lead. Mutually they explored each other's sensitive zones.

Crystal was more treasured than her name. Brett valued each kiss as a token of her love freely given. The restraint he had used to end their previous encounters was pitiful when compared to the control necessary to keep from plunging into her inviting warmth and driving away the tightening ache in his loins.

When she frantically, frenziedly raked her nails down the length of Brett's smooth back, he entered her, stroking her heated flesh.

The flaming colors she had seen before were sparked into a psychedelic pattern. They swirled, circled, and blended, changing from pure tones to vibrant hues: blue to turquoise, deep green became lime colored, the yellow lightened and brightened as it soared over the darker colors.

No longer was she setting the tempo. Nature's oldest rhythm orchestrated their movement. With each deep thrust Crystal murmured his name in a mindless litany. As his stroking quickened, his name was no longer inaudible. To her own ears, to Brett's, to the earth and the sun beyond, she shouted his name triumphantly.

She had given everything a woman has: love, desire, passion.

Lifting his weight to his knees and elbows, Brett nuzzled the dusty rose peaks of her breasts with ragged breaths.

Crystal's eyes opened. Passion flecked her irises with gold. Their hips still locked, her eyes widened at the realization that not only had Brett taken her to glorious heights, he had restrained from easing his own physical need.

"Brett?" she questioned in awe. For a moment she felt despair. Had she been such a poor lover that he had been unable to reach the pinnacle she had clung to?

"No. Not for that reason," he said, divining her thought and halting her runaway doubts. "You're precious to me, love. Too precious to take a chance."

Lost in ecstasy, she hadn't thought of the possible consequences of their loving. Mentally she calculated the possibility of this being a fertile time of the month. Biting her lip, she refigured, knowing it was. Hands on the bedspread, she began wriggling their hips apart. Perhaps it wasn't too late if he hadn't . . .

His hands prevented their separating by clasping her squirming hips. "Relax. Lean over and get the box from the top drawer of the nightstand," he instructed soothingly.

"I want you to have my sons and daughters, but not until you're ready," he said softly, taking care of the precautionary measures deftly. "But now I need the heat of your inner fire. We'll burn together this time," he promised.

Chapter Nine

Totally depleted of energy, Crystal wanted nothing more than to sleep. Exactly the opposite of what all the articles she had read said should be happening. Supposedly, they should be exchanging love talk, chattering like magpies in a cage. The warm glow of love surrounding and enveloping her made speech impossible. Brett would understand, wouldn't he?

A gnawing ache in her stomach grew into a full-fledged low rumbling growl. Crystal stretched.

"That is some alarm clock you have," Brett joshed, his hand loitering between the delicate oval of her navel and the valley of her breasts.

"I'm starving. You did promise a drink and lunch," she complained petulantly. With a wink she added, "You're supposed to wine and dine *before* seducing."

His face hovered above her. She framed the

carved bones, thumbs drawing the corners of his lips upward. Did all women believe the man they loved was the epitome of handsomeness? Or was it an affliction peculiar to herself? Remembering the two office workers in the park, she knew the answer.

He was, a cluster of adjectives slipped through her lips, *"attractive, masculine,"* Stroking one finger over his naturally arched eyebrow, she continued: *"rugged, virile."* Her hands lightly skimmed his shoulders— *"athletic,"*—then lowered—"and *lusty*."

Fingering the good-luck unicorn, his grin widened with each compliment. "Seductress, you tempt me to lock the door and keep you prisoner." Using the teeny hooves of the mythological ivory beast, he traced the bow of her lips. "Hungry enough to eat a horse?"

"Not that one," she mumbled. "Beefsteak. Thick, juicy, rare, with a baked potato swamped in sour cream and a salad with everything in it but the kitchen sink."

"A man's meal...meat and poatoes."

"I've burned up scads of calories," she replied, swatting his behind. 'I'm faint from hunger."

"Message received. Off and on, woman."

"Off and on?" she quizzed, unfamiliar with the slang.

"Off your beautifully rounded tush and onto

your dainty feet.'' The stinging slap on her derriere emphasized the explanation.

Bounding off the bed, Crystal laughed and headed toward the closed door. Brett sprang off the mattress, heading toward the door they had entered earlier. When Crystal rushed into the walk-in closet, she realized why Brett was laughing.

"You are no gentleman, Mr. Masterson,'' she shouted, chagrined by her logistical error.

From the short hallway she heard the volume of his boisterous laughter increase. The steady splatter of running water and loud singing led her to the bathroom. Brett was already in the shower. Through the opaque glass she saw him, back to the shower nozzle, soaping and rinsing.

With the stealth of a cat burglar she cracked the sliding-glass door, reached in, and shut off the hot water. The yelping and mild expletives coming from the stall were music to her ears. Gleefully she laughed at the success of the prank. Two seconds later she was bodily hauled into the shower and stuck under the cold spray.

"Brett . . . my hair,'' she squealed. "It's freezing!''

"Say *uncle*.''

"Uncle! Uncle!''

Immediately the hot water was restored.

"I'll lay money you pulled that stunt a hundred times on your poor brother," he said, chuckling. "Too bad he couldn't return the favor the way I did."

"I'll probably get pneumonia, and it will all be your fault."

Brett's soapy hands skimmed over her front. "We'll both be sick. A week in bed, snuggled under the covers, devoting all our energy to thinking up ways to keep from being bored." The gentle hands lathering her upper thighs assured her what sort of games they would be playing.

"I accept the invitation. Turn off the hot water," she replied saucily, reaching toward the knob herself.

"Hussy."

Crystal wiggled against him provocatively.

"I'll give you an hour to stop that," Brett said, wrapping her closer, fingers splaying over the tips of her breasts.

"In an hour I'll be able to compete with a prune . . . and win."

Groaning, aroused, Brett swept her hair aside and kissed the hollowed V inside her collar bone before lifting the weight of her hair, twisting it, and holding it on the crown of her head. "Turn," he instructed, splashing the water and rinsing the lather off.

Revolving slowly, Crystal flushed from the neck upward when she realized how uninhibitedly and wantonly she was behaving. Who would believe she had been raised in a family that hadn't allowed pajamas and robes at the breakfast table? *You've come a long way, baby.*

"Mmmm. Body beautiful," Brett said appreciatively.

Did he really mean that? Hardly. Crystal was still surprised when she smiled in front of a mirror and her teeth weren't covered with wire. Brett was probably saying the things he thought she wanted to hear.

The steamy spray ceased abruptly. She felt her damp hair fall, spilling over her back to the tip of her spine. Hypnotizing eyes were enticing her to close the scant inches between their bodies.

"My idea of a feast is licking each and every drop of water off you." The deep timbre of his voice, laced with desire, sent a shiver of goosebumps up her arms.

Brett slid the shower door back, nudging her out. With a navy-blue towel he gently wiped the water from her back.

Spinning her around, he said, "Next time I'll—"

"Let me have the shower first?" Crystal interrupted pertly. Brett dropped to one knee, casting her a wicked grin. "Don't you enjoy this?" he asked. Starting at her ankle, he worked his way up to the juncture of her upper thighs.

The moments it took to complete the task were filled with erotic thoughts of the ecstasy they had shared earlier. Eyes closed, her head was spinning dizzily as he twisted her to complete the toweling process.

"Get dressed," he told her quickly, toweling himself. "I'm going to have a quick shave to get rid of my five o'clock shadow."

Blinking, Crystal cleared her mind of sensual thoughts. One glance at Brett revealed his desire, but it was tempered by his iron control. Exiting, she wondered how he could touch every wet inch of skin on her body and not carry her back to bed. An ounce of his self-control was pounds more than she had, she acknowledged silently.

An hour later Crystal was comfortably replete from a delicious pasta dinner at a small family-run Italian restaurant. Their empty plates had been removed and she slumped deeper into the tufted leather seat of the booth, crossing her legs at the knees.

"Any complaints about the change of menu?" Brett queried in a low voice.

"I'll never request steak and potatoes again," she groaned, rubbing her taut stomach.

"Care to go back to my place for a night-cap?" he offered, running his hand over her thigh beneath the white-linen tablecloth.

Crystal smiled wickedly. Turning, lips mere inches from his ear, she whispered sultrily, "Romp in the hay... mad, passionate love, maybe... but calling it a nightcap is a new twist."

Brushing a lock of hair behind her ear, he replied, "You're being very provocative, love. A few more words of that nature and we won't be allowed back in here." His fingers tightened significantly on her swinging knee. "How am I going to find out about you when I'm distracted by—"

"I'll behave," she replied with mock haughtiness. Scooting to the left, she dislodged his hand. I'll be as suave as he is, she promised herself. "What do you want to know?"

"Everything. The things you like, or hate. Your favorite color, celestial sign, food, hobbies, et cetera, et cetera."

"I like dark eyes caressing—"

"Crystal!" Brett reprimanded, then laughed.

"Wrong answer?"

"Right answer, but provocative again."

"Mmm-kay," she agreed, wanting to find out the small pieces of information she would be able to coax out of him in return.

The next hour was spent sipping coffee, swapping trivial tidbits, and laughing. Crystal was surprised at the number of things they had in common. When they did disagree Brett quietly listened to her point of view, then precisely, logically presented his views. She carefully skirted any subjects that had caused dissension in the past, and Brett obliged also. If the discussion threatened to become a heated argument, he changed the subject.

Too soon they left the restaurant and the cocoon of the car. Hand in hand they strolled up the sidewalk in front of her apartment. During the drive Brett had asked her out for the following evening. Readily she had accepted.

Mac and Scotty barked from the fenced-in patio. Being 'people dogs,' they disliked being left out of doors after dark.

"Shhhh," Crystal shushed. The shrill yipping was not conducive to prolonged leave-taking at the front door.

"Come on in, Brett. They missed their evening run," she explained while unlocking the door and hurrying to the patio doors.

Both dogs leaped past Crystal and dashed toward the still-open front door. Seeing their intent, Brett quickly stepped inside and shut it.

"It's too late for you to walk them. Why don't I take them for a short run," he offered, squatting down to pet each dog vigorously.

"Thanks. I'd appreciate it." She assumed he was doing the gentlemanly thing, giving her time to slip into something more comfortable. "Get your coats, boys."

Seconds later, leashes dragging behind them, tails wagging furiously, they reentered. Crystal slipped their coats into place.

"They're well trained," Brett complimented, chuckling at their hind quarters, which were bouncing and wagging in anticipation.

"All my men are," Crystal teased. "Actually, training them is easy." Her voice trailed off, leading Brett to inquire further.

Eyes twinkling, he said, "I'll bite. What is the secret of your phenomenal success?"

Handing him the leashes, she said succinctly, "Chocolate-chip cookies. They love 'em."

"Me, too," he confided. "I have the world's greatest craving for something . . . sweet." Opening the door, he grinned broadly and quipped, "Be right back . . . sweetheart."

Racing into her bedroom, Crystal decided quickly which nightgown she would wear. Pulling open the bottom drawer of the triple dresser, she unwrapped the lacy blue confection from the tissue paper she had stored it in. Grinning, she remembered feeling foolish when she had purchased it. The entire bodice was the sheerest of cobweb lace and the remainder was nearly as transparent. It was special. One she had saved.

Disrobing, she donned the gown and put on the matching slippers. She brushed her long hair until the golden highlights shone; a spritz of Tatiana on the pulse points completed her toiletry just as she heard the door click shut.

"Crystal?" Brett called from the living room.

Hastily she decided to be lounging on the bed with the dim light from the bathroom spilling into the room.

"In here," she answered, ready.

Brett stopped in the doorway. For long moments he was absolutely still. Then, ever so slowly, he crossed to the edge of the bed.

"You are the most desirable woman I've ever met," he praised her huskily. Kneeling beside the bed, raising her palm to his lips, he said solemnly, "I love you. I love the woman who entices me with her softness. I love the child whose pranks make me feel young and carefree. What we have dreams are made of." His lips trailed up to the bend of her elbow and planted a moist, warm kiss at the bend. His smoldering eyes watched the tips of her breasts become taut under the transparent lace.

"Sometimes it scares me to touch you." Tentatively his fingertips lightly touched her brown-rimmed nipples. "I keep thinking to myself, this is too beautiful to be real...." His dark eyes locked with hers." And then you do something that makes it more beautiful."

"It is dreamlike. I struggled trying to keep you at a distance, but couldn't. I'm the moth; you're the flame."

"Irresistible forces?"

As she nodded in agreement, her hair fell over one slender shoulder, drawing dark eyes to the sheer bodice and the rounded cleavage awaiting his touch. They honed in on the ivory charm.

Following his gaze, Crystal touched the charm. Seeing the clasp had slipped around to the front, she automatically began inching it up toward her collarbone. His warm hand halted the movement. A dark, strange intensity mesmerized her fingertips. Bending to his will, they unlatched the safety clasp. Brett had given so much of himself. She was compelled to give also.

The golden thread fell into her hand. Eyes brimming with love, Crystal reached behind his neck and hooked the latch together. The ivory unicorn nestled in its new home on the dark plains of his chest as if it had always been there.

The burning gleam flared brighter when Brett said huskily, "If I never love again, I'll have had today. Love me, Crystal. Long into the night . . . early into the morning."

Chapter Ten

Each day for the next two weeks belonged to Brett. Crystal's mind was with him during the day; body and soul were his at night. Being organized and goal-oriented were the only factors making functioning at work possible.

The E.B.S. article was shaping up nicely. The pictures met Mike's requirements, and graphically pointed out the difference in the male human form. She wanted to use Brett's pictures, but knew it was out of the question. In a short space of time she had taken impromptu snaps of him hundreds of times. He was her favorite model...the epitome of E.B.S. His photographs lined the darkroom, bedroom, and had managed to form a small pile on her desk.

Putting the final touches on the written part of the story, Crystal leaned back in her chair, feeling a glow of satisfaction. The reader would be hard-pressed not to smile at the tongue-in-cheek message: Ladies, open your eyes and enjoy the E.B.S. scenery around you. The dialogue in the script generally was quotes of comments the men had made when asked to sign the releases. Skimming the captions below the pictures, she grinned.

"Bold women are a turn on."

"Like it? Touch it."

"E.B.S. need T.L.C."

Crystal particularly liked the shot of a less-than-firm bottom in a warm-up suit. The tilted handlebar mustache said more than the few words below: *Love handles.* Mike had finally approved the collage of photos for the cover of the magazine. One lapping over the other artistically were shots of a wide range of eyes, masculine shoulders, and male posteriors.

Surprisingly, considering his ultraconservative viewpoint, Brett had jovially accompanied her on many of the picture-finding safaris. His relaxed attitude had been taxed only once.

She had been snapping a picture of brawny male shoulders at a gymnasium. Intent on getting the right angle, she was unaware of her own jean-clad derriere being focused on by a muscle-bound he-man behind her. Completing her task, she pivoted to return to Brett's side and nearly dropped her teeth. Her protector was toe to toe, belly to belly, with a man out-weighing and towering over him.

"Stop it!" she remembered shouting. "Brett!"

"You tell 'im, lady. I didn't mean no harm," the weight lifter said ungrammatically.

"Apologize to the *lady,*" Brett spat out be-tween clenched teeth.

"I'm sorry, already. I didn't mean nuthin'."

Firmly clasping Crystal by the arm, Brett hus-tled her out to the parking lot. Not wanting to cause a scene or further humiliation, she al-lowed herself to be pulled along like a puppy on a leash.

Beside the car she demanded, "What the hell is wrong with you? You made me look like an idiot!"

"I didn't make you look like an idiot. You managed to do that without any assistance." Unlocking the door on the Cadillac, he pushed her into the car and strode to the driver's side.

"Taking pictures does not make me an idiot. Keep your hands off me and my camera. Of all the..."

She wasn't allowed to finish her tirade. Firm lips clamped over hers, grinding the soft inner flesh against her teeth. She was tempted to sink her pointed teeth into the tip of his hard prob-ing tongue, but resisted the impulse. Nothing in their relationship had prepared her for the rib-crushing embrace or the fury of his kiss. It was over before she could respond or fight.

"I will not allow any man to make suggestive hand signals, drawing a crowd, when *you* are the object. It disgusts me." The disdainful, bitter words spewed from his mouth.

Never one to back down from a fight or be bullied, Crystal fought back.

"Why you stiff-necked, brittle snob! What could he have done in the midst of a crowd?"

"Embarrass you."

"Why let a stranger embarrass me? I brought *you* along," she sarcastically flung at him. "From now on, Mister Straighter-than-an-arrow don't interfere. Butt out!"

"I know. You can take care of yourself," he snorted, mimicking her favorite phrase. "There are times and situations when *most* women would appreciate having a man to protect them."

"Back in the eighteen hundreds, yes. But the man had two empty hands . . . not a tomahawk, and he wasn't going to scalp me!"

"Maybe not, but his intentions were far from honorable. I stopped him before he could *feel* what he had been admiring."

"I've been pinched before and survived," Crystal muttered. "Turn right at the next street. I want to go home . . . alone."

"Is this our first lovers' quarrel?" Brett asked, a beguiling smile twitching at the corners of his lips.

Crystal shot him an icy glare, which by all rights should have killed the laughter he was suppressing.

"I said turn right," she insisted, when he blithely drove past the street. "All right then ... stop the car; I'll take a cab!"

Silence.

"Kidnapping is a federal offense. I mean it, Brett! Stop the car!"

Instantly the car swerved to the right and Brett tromped on the brake, pitching her dangerously forward. The door latch barely touched her fingertips when she felt herself lifted up, her head unintentionally whacked against the ceiling of the car, and implanted on his lap.

"Let's make up," he suggested, contained laughter rumbling in his chest. "I hear it's the best part of open warfare." Crystal struggled, kicking her legs and twisting to get away. "I love teasing you. You're like a puppy with his hackles up."

Clumsily she tried to untangle herself from the magnetic warmth of Brett and the unrelenting pressure of the steering wheel gouging her back. It was an exercise in futility. The wheel wouldn't budge, and Brett wouldn't either. The squirming and scuffling was too reminiscent of the love play on his king-size bed. Inevitably their love play would end in soaring passion, ignited by the friction of their bodies rubbing against each other like matches on emery paper.

Not this time, she vowed. She had to make a stand and stick by it. How was she going to make him understand she could handle awkward situations? At all costs she must not fall under the spell of his magical hands this time.

"Going to play hard to get?" Brett asked, running teasing fingers up her rib cage. "The curb of a busy street is not the place to issue a challenge."

Impassively, limply, Crystal replied, "No games. No challenges. Please take me home."

The heat from his gaze tried to pierce her icy armor, but she was determined not to give in. The incident in the gymnasium was indicative of the male possessiveness he was beginning to practice in regard to her. Crystal wanted equality in their relationship. Loving Brett shouldn't change an independent, free-thinking, self-sufficient woman into a groveling, sniveling worm.

How did he expect her to react to being jerked out of the gym and thrown into his car?

What did he expect? An apology for something she had not asked for or encouraged? Bullroar! Letting him walk on her now would lead to a big ruckus later. He had best understand *now* she wasn't going to be dominated by any man . . . regardless of how much she loved him.

He didn't cajole or berate Crystal any further. Nor did he apologize. Releasing her, he silently followed her command and took her home.

"Call me when you've cooled off and come to your senses," he instructed at her doorstep.

Her first impulse, when she saw him climbing back into his car, was to chase after him and fling herself into his arms, or under his front tires if necessary, to stop his departure. But the word *equality* stiffened her backbone. There was a principle involved, she told herself.

"You'll have to call me, mister," she growled.

In the week since their argument, Brett had still not called. The glow of satisfaction at having the E.B.S. article ready for Mike waned. Reaching into her bottom desk drawer, Crystal pulled out the manila envelope that housed Brett's pictures. She undid the clasp, and they spilled out.

Put them away, her mind ordered. *You're weakening*.

Eyeing the telephone, hand moving toward

it, she tried to recall the principle she was fighting for. What could she say if she did call him? I'm a weak-kneed, lily-livered woman in desperate need of love and affection?

Crystal shook her head. Her pink, oval fingertip traced lightly over the glossy black-and-white of Brett bending down to pick a rose from beside the flower bed. She remembered his touching the stamen of the flaming red flower and putting the finely powdered pollen behind her ear. Automatically her hand reached for the small unicorn. It was gone too. She had given him everything: her heart, her body, her soul...her good-luck piece.

Head jerking up, she schooled her face into an icy mask when Chad stomped into their office. The scowl he tossed in her direction did not penetrate the hard shell she had erected around herself.

"You couldn't settle for second best. Nooooo; Miss-Goodie-Two-Shoes wants it all." Lip snarling, curling upward, his voice lowered menacingly. "You're in big trouble now, lady. Enjoy your next assignment. You'll be fired before it's in print."

The telephone buzzing stopped the poisonous vilification. Chad picked it up, eyes turning to steely flint as he listened.

"Yes, sir. She's on her way." The receiver

hovered, then slammed home. "Mike wants you. I'm to be the messenger boy sent to production with the E.B.S. story. You'll regret stepping on *my* toes, Crystal Lake."

Composure intact, Crystal arose and strode to the door. The animosity between them finally in the open, she was spurred into smiling broadly and delivering a short, ego-killing blow. "Grow up . . . *boy*."

Chad sputtered, jumped to his feet, and stormed toward her, open palm raised.

"Striking a co-worker will get *you* fired. Go ahead," she blustered, thrusting out her chin to receive the blow, "hit me."

Killing looks were exchanged across the limited space between them. As his hand dropped to his side in slow motion, Crystal's jaw relaxed.

A surge of adrenaline flushed through her system. She had won. She didn't know how or why, but some way she had defeated Chad.

Grinning, she left the small enclosure they shared and with a light, carefree step crossed the main office, oblivious to the smiling faces of the office staff.

Seeing Mike hunched over his desk, sorting through a stack of papers, made the smile widen. The old devil knew Chad was mad enough to spit nails into steel girders, but was, as always, too professional to allow in-house personal conflicts to affect the well-oiled machinery of the magazine's wheel.

"About time you got here," Mike said in his usual gravelly voice. "The day-care story has the green light from the higher ups."

Crystal felt like jumping up and down, clapping her hands in joy, and flinging her arms around Mike's neck and planting a humungous kiss on his cheek. He had to have given his personal support for this article, or it would have been dropped down the tubes into oblivion, as a multitude of other hot-potato stories had.

"You can come back to earth," he continued, shaggy brows drawn down as his forehead wrinkled. "There is a catch. Private industry is the target, not public utilities." Mike shoved a list of companies toward her as she leaned forward in her seat.

"That changes the whole thrust of the idea," she stated.

"Agreed. The principle remains the same: Working mothers need on-site day care. The powers that be want to encourage the private sector to assume responsibilities, *if* you can convince them in the first section of the story there is a legitimate need."

"Well, it's a start," she conceded. "I would have preferred the meaty gristle and grit of investigating the fat padding of public utilities. This will turn out to be a milk and honey story, won't it?"

Mike's hand hid a grin. "Maybe we should put you back in the gourmet section of *SLM*. First buns ... now milk and honey." A chuckle escaped his throat.

"A protein-deficient diet," Crystal tossed back. "Try adding *meat* to make it well balanced."

"Meat being synonymous with public and governmental employers?"

"Right on!"

"Then consider yourself a vegetarian," he quipped.

"I need something to sink my teeth into."

"No meat," Mike stressed, concluding the discussion.

Crystal shrugged, stood, jammed her hands in her jacket pockets, and rattled some loose change.

"Hear that?" she asked sweetly. "Dentures! Pardon me while I toddle on out of here and *gum* another article together."

Mike laughed. "Keep the quality of your work improving and gradually you'll be weaned off milk and honey." His hand gestured for her to remain in the office. "Speaking of food, Jane is making mother-hen noises about not seeing you lately. Does Cousin Brett have you booked, or can you both come to dinner Saturday night?"

"Brett hasn't called lately." Crystal paused.

This was the excuse she was looking for. She could call Brett without crawling. What could be better than a joint invitation issued by his relative? "Why don't I check to see what's on his agenda and give Jane a buzz later today?"

"She's enjoying the prospect of matchmaking. Be warned," Mike answered, shaking his head at the whimsical notion of matching Crystal up with anybody.

"I'd trust her with my most intimate secrets."

"It's not *your* secrets I worry about," he replied caustically.

Crystal grinned, recalling Mike instructing his wife to keep her mouth shut when they had teased him about his buns.

"We're barbecuing. You want your steak rare?"

"Same as always, of course."

"Bring your dentures," Mike added wryly to the rare-meat joke.

Crystal folded the list of companies and jingled her way out of the office. Seeing the backside of Chad vanishing in the stairwell and knowing she did not have to face another head-to-head confrontation added to the spring in her step. With him out of the way she could call Brett immediately.

Her finger trembled while dialing his number at work. Thousands of reasons for him to reject the dinner invitation nudged the back of her mind.

"Negative thinking," she muttered into the mouthpiece as the dialed numbers musically toned in her ear. "He will accept," she muttered between each ring.

"Hello, Brett?" she asked, knowing it was the number directly into his office.

"Crystal?"

"Yes," she responded, unable to say more until she swallowed twice to dislodge the lump that hearing his voice had brought to her throat. "How are you?"

"Better now," he answered. Crystal envisioned the fires warming his eyes as he spoke.

Plunging right in, she said, "Mike and Jane have invited us to dinner Saturday night. Can you make it?"

She could hear him flipping the pages on his desk calendar. Silently she prayed the page would be blank. It had to be.

"What would you do if I played hard to get and told you the evening was booked?"

Shoot myself, she thought silently before asking, "Is it?"

"No."

Releasing the air held in her lungs, her heart had room to function again and thumped loudly. "Devil!" she accused, smiling.

"Did you miss me?" Brett asked softly.

"Have you been gone?" she asked, repaying him in kind for his stalled reply.

"M.I.A. Missing in Action. I wasn't defeated; I retreated."

"The invitation was an excuse to call. I've had my hand on the phone all week," she admitted.

Brett gave a pleased chuckle. "For once your bluntness is working for me." His voice lowered to a touch above a whisper. "*Did* you miss me?"

"Terribly. Will you come over tonight?"

"I have a meeting scheduled," he said, almost groaning in frustration. "Can I come by afterward?"

"Yes," she answered eagerly. "Will it be late?"

"Not if I know you're waiting."

"I'm not the only one who's missed you. Are you ready for a few wet, slurpy kisses?"

"Scotty and Mac?" he questioned in a light voice.

Crystal laughed. "Your fictitious competitors of the past have also missed you."

"Tell them it's their night on the sofa."

"For the past few nights Scotty has put his forepaws on the edge of the bed and checked out the contents before jumping in. Then he rests his head on my knee and sighs dramatically." The brief episode could have been told about me, she thought silently, remembering her own deep sighs of longing and misery.

"Sounds as though they've switched sides, doesn't it?"

"You men always stick together," she complained with a smile in her voice. "A poor, defenseless woman doesn't stand a chance."

"You're a victim of cupboard love. Scotty and Mac have a weakness I converted into a weapon for my side."

"Brett Masterson, have you been bribing my dogs with chocolate-chip cookies?" she asked with mock ferocity, twisting the coiled phone cord around her hand.

"I reversed the 'Love me, love my dog,' theory. The way to a woman's heart is through her pets' sweet tooth."

Laughing at his disclosure, Crystal realized how he had used every scrap of information he knew to bind them together. It really was the work of a master strategist. She also silently admitted enjoying the single-minded thrust of . . . being seduced. Her laughter died at the admission. Their differences still existed. Passion, desire, even love would have difficulty overcoming the obstacles the fates had placed between them.

"What's wrong?" Brett asked as her laughter dwindled into silence.

"Nothing," Crystal lied, not wanting her thoughts to blight the prospects for the evening. "I was calculating how much it's going to cost you to take the dogs to the dentist when their teeth fall out."

"Do Keebler's little elves make sugar-free cookies?" he teased. "I'll have to check it out at the grocery store. Can't have my troops in anything but the best of health." Brett paused. "I'll see you tonight," he promised. "Talking on the phone is no substitute for holding you." The laughter had disappeared from his voice. "I'm afraid the words, or the inflection in my voice, will punch your eject button and I'll find myself out in the cold."

"I'll see you later," she replied, ending the conversation but gripping the phone tighter.

"Till later," he agreed.

Crystal waited for the sound of his receiver to click as it was returned to its base. Hearing his voice carried by twisted wires buried under the paved streets of St. Louis had an intimacy all its own. Her honey-toned eyes inspected the mouthpiece as she held it near the desktop. For some unknown reason she didn't want to be the one to break contact.

"I love you," she whispered softly, not knowing whether or not he heard the declaration.

Chapter Eleven

I *should* be docked a day's wages, Crystal thought as she opened her apartment door. Brett Masterson had occupied her mind the entire day. She'd have to get her priorities back in line or she would make Chad the happiest man on staff when she received a pink slip in her pay envelope.

The first assignment with any grit at all, and she had wasted the day mooning around the office like an adolescent. Her single accomplishment for the day had been taking the list Mike had given her and making appointments for interviews. Not exactly a day she could mark down the calendar as productive.

"Come on in, you traitorous lops," Crystal said, sliding open the patio door.

Scotty and Mac barked excitedly, making a miniature racetrack around her feet. Crystal

bent down and swooped Scotty into her arms.
His four feet, still in rapid movement, slowed
as she rubbed his pointed ears and thumped his
sides with love pats. Small, round dark eyes
sparkled with mischievousness.

"I know your secret. You formed an alliance
with Brett. Those sighs at night are caused by
sugar withdrawal, you rascal."

Scotty's stubby tail wiggled against Crystal's
rib cage. Mac, even jealous, began jumping two
feet off the carpet. Putting Scotty down, she
picked up Mac.

"I know. You always think you need your
loving first." A pink tongue licked near, but
not on, her cheek. Both dogs knew she hated
being slobbered on and politely refrained from
dog-washing her face. "Okay. Down you go."
Shaking her finger in their direction, she said
laughingly, "No more fraternizing with Brett."
Sitting on their haunches, heads cocked, they
listened as though they understood every word.
Seeing their tails wagging, she could tell they
had vetoed her instructions.

After straightening the apartment and eating,
she made the final decision as to what to wear
for the evening and laid it out on the bed. Her
eyes swept over the gold satin, two-piece lounging pajamas. It was an outfit she had worn before, which Brett had described as what every

well-dressed officer in the military should wear. It was a compliment, disguised by their running military dialogue.

Glancing at her watch and noting the time made her spring into action. Humming a string of favorite love ballads, Crystal showered, applied a light coat of makeup, brushed her hair until it glistened, and slipped into the seductive softness of the satin pajamas.

"Not bad," she commented, appraising the total effect in a full-length mirror. "What do you think, boys?" she asked the dogs, who were stretched out beside the bed, watching her every move. "Don't answer; you're biased. You should have seen me a few years back. A scrawny scarecrow would have beat me in a beauty contest."

Scotty walked to the mirror. Peering at his own reflection, his tail moved faster than a printing press.

"You egotistical beast," Crystal reproved. "You're supposed to be admiring me, not yourself."

Scotty snorted.

Shrugging her shoulders, Crystal muttered, "You get a doggy bone instead of a cookie."

Instantly Scotty sat up on his hind legs, begging at the mention of the treat, Crystal could almost swear she saw a grin on his face.

"Living alone is taking its toll on my sanity," she mumbled to her reflection.

Sitting in front of the television, leafing through a past edition of *SLM*, Crystal waited. She tried to concentrate on something other than the slow-moving hands of the clock and drifted into conjecturing what Brett's intention for the evening would be. An impish smile curved her lips upward as she hoped his intentions would be anything but honorable.

The past week of longing and loneliness had provided her with time to reconsider his proposal. Loving Brett, which she readily accepted as a fact, should lead to the permanent commitment he wanted. Crystal squirmed.

The written list she had made of the pros and cons of marriage had more items to the left than the right. The truth glared her in the face. It wasn't Brett who was deficient; it was herself.

By making the list she had done exactly what he had accused her of: viewed life in black and white. Justifying her philosophy, she muttered to herself, "It's the grays in our relationship that muddle the clarity of the picture."

The fight they had had over his possessive behavior at the gymnasium was the type of problem she felt they could work out. With time he would learn how far he could encroach upon the territory she felt he had no right to invade. The key word was *time*. Perhaps, in time, if she could control her temper, and if he didn't hassle her about her job, then maybe, *just maybe,* they could consider making a commitment to each other.

The chiming of the door bell ended her introspection. Her heart accelerating, she opened the door before the second ring. All logical thoughts were banished when she looked at the strongly chiseled lines of fatigue on his face. In the dark his eyes glowed as they silently skimmed over her.

Arms extended, she welcomed him. Wordlessly, in the language of lovers, she folded herself against him. Inexplicably Crystal felt a tear slip to the lapel of his dark suit when she snuggled closer. Pressing her nose against his shirt, she smelled the essence of the man she loved with every bone, muscle, blood cell in her body.

"You're where you belong," Brett murmured, his warm, minty breath feathering her temple.

The friction of nodding her head against the polished silk of his shirt made her skin tingle. Withdrawing, her arm remaining around his waist, she led him into the living room.

"How did the meeting go?" she asked.

Brett smiled. "Slowly."

Grinning back at him, she remembered her social graces. "Drink?"

His smiling gaze dropped from her eyes to her lips. "Um-hmm," he replied, his lips slightly vibrating as they closed over hers.

The taste of his questing tongue was more refreshing than a mint julep on a sultry summer day. Deepening the kiss, he drank in the honeyed sweetness she offered. Arms lifting, winding around, circling him in love, she pressed herself against him. Her chest was pressed against his unbuttoned jacket, and satin and silk sensually massaged her rounded breasts exotically. The guttural sound from deep in his throat as he cupped her hips and tenderly brought them against his unmistakable masculine arousal brought an echoing sigh. Her thirst could not be quenched by merely kissing.

"Brett," she said between panting breaths as he strung, hot moist kisses on her arched neck, "come love me."

"God, I want to. I want to," he mumbled against the pulse rapidly throbbing against his lips. "I can't."

Can't? her mind shrieked in disbelief. Twisting at the hips, she knew his body was making a liar out of his denial.

"Yes," she coaxed, lips outlining the shell of his ear, then nipping the lobe with a love bite.

"Won't."

His hands slackened their hold. Crystal clung to his shoulders, refusing to let his won't-power dictate to his desire. Brett peeled her away. Pride wounded, her arms limply dropped to her sides. Swiveling away, she blinked rapidly to keep the moisture threatening to overflow from being seen.

How could he say no? It wasn't as though they had never made love. Had her wanton, abandoned plea turned him off? Folding her arms across her chest, she falteringly stepped to the sofa and collapsed into its softness. Eyes closed, salty tears swam down the back of her throat. She didn't know where Brett was. Nor did she care. Controlling her quaking emotions required absolute consolidation of all five senses. The flames of passion converted into the heat of anger.

"That was despicable," Crystal spat. "Men have foul names for women who lead them on. What's the reverse equivalent?"

Opening her eyes, she found herself delivering the words to Brett's stiff back. The urge to pitch the table lamp against his shoulder blades made her fist clamp shut. Acting in a juvenile fashion would only confirm what a fool she had been.

Her long fingers raked over the back of

Brett's well-shaped head, then clamped on the back of his neck.

"The word you're searching for is *bastard*...in capital letters," he muttered in self-deprecating tone. "I didn't mean for things to get out of control."

"Damn your control," Crystal hissed.

Pivoting, hand jammed in his pockets, his eyes bore into hers as he advanced to the sofa. Obstinately she glared back.

"For weeks you've been using me," he stated levelly. Reaching into his jacket pocket, he extracted a green-velvet jeweler's box and tossed it on the sofa cushion between them as he sat down.

Tentatively she reached toward it, then clamped her hand back on her upper arm. *An engagement ring* circled and spun in her mind.

Sexual tension was replaced by suppressed anger on both their parts.

"Scared?" he taunted. "It's yours. Keep it... throw it away... accept it as payment for services rendered."

Digging her fingernails into her own flesh, she kept from wiping the spiteful remark off his face with the palm of her hand.

"I won't be insulted in my own home. Loving you was the biggest mistake I've ever made in my life."

"Love?" he derided. "You don't know the meaning of the word. *Passion,* yes. *Sex,* yes. *Love?* uh-uh."

"Get out, Brett," she whispered. "Get out before I say something I'll regret."

"Not this time, lady. When you run out of names to hurl at me, I'm going to be sitting right here waiting. It's time to cut the crap and get down to the bottom line. Why won't you marry me?"

"You've known all along I didn't want a permanent relationship," she spat.

"Why?"

"We don't fit together," she explained, emphasizing each word.

"Five minutes ago we fit together very nicely."

"Now who's confusing love and sex?" she retorted scathingly.

"I stand corrected. At least on that point we agree. We are sexually compatible. How are we not compatible?"

Crystal lowered her eyes. "You hate my job. In fact, basically you dislike the idea of women having a career."

"Don't twist what I've said. We're wading in mud as it is. Your job isn't the problem. As to the second statement, you've generalized again. I don't object to the mass of women in the work force. Most of them are there to support their families. Specifically, as in our case, your working wouldn't be financially necessary."

"What would I do all day while you're out earning a living? Take up knitting?"

"There is a multitude of choices. When we touched on this subject over a month ago, I told you money doesn't restrict; it liberates. Surely there are activities you are interested in that could occupy your time."

Unfolding one arm, Crystal slammed it into the seat cushion. "I occupy my time with a career I just happen to be particularly fond of. Working isn't a drudgery performed to pay the bills."

"Do free-lance work. Then *you* select the topic instead of being stuck with an assignment you find repugnant."

"You mean an assignment *you* find repugnant," she retorted. "The E.B.S. story turned out to be fun."

Brett shook his head. Exasperation lined his face, dragging the corners of his lips downward. "We can come to an amicable agreement about your work. You're tossing out red herrings. What's the real problem?"

Crystal focused on the dogs peering through the nose prints smudged on the patio door.

Grabbing her best excuse to end the discussion, she began rising from the sofa. The jeweler's case slipped to the floor. Brett's fingers clamped around her wrist like velvet handcuffs. Bending forward, he retrieved the box.

"Open it," he commanded, firmly wrapping her loose fingers around it.

Her dark hair swirled over her slender shoulders as she vigorously shook her head. The litany she had practiced for ten years burst forth, "I am a career woman. I want to remain free."

"A continuation of the love affair," he surmised, dark eyes narrowing to a pinpoint of light smaller than a laser beam.

"Yes," she replied softly. "You know I love you ... want you. Why must there be more?" The beguiling liquid honey of her eyes flowed over him.

Sighing heavily in defeat, Brett stroked her hand. "Open the gift. It isn't a ring." As if he knew she didn't believe him, Brett opened it for her.

Crystal gasped in pleasure when she saw the contents. The ivory unicorn was nestled on a bed of cotton. In its mouth was the smallest, most perfectly formed rose with a teeny black gem winking from its center.

"Oh, Brett, it's exquisite. Thank you."

The hard pebble of a core in her heart

that prevented her from any commitment was touched. The artistic blending of both of their good-luck symbols was indicative of his sensitive nature. She was literally choked up with tenderness.

"You never did tell me why you touched the inside of a flower, then put the powder behind my ear."

Pollen is part of the fertilization process. Some cultures believe it is an aphrodisiac." Lifting the fragile chain and charm, he circled it gently around her neck.

The unicorn dropped into place in the shadowed valley between her breasts, and at the same moment Brett strung kisses on the nape of her neck. Slowly turning her, he followed the threadlike thickness of the golden chain down the provocative V. The warm moistness of his breath sealed the chain to the softness of her skin.

Between nibbles and kisses Brett whispered, "You're mine. Would you be the mother of my children?"

"Children?" Crystal repeated, her voice squeaking.

"Small, dark-haired, independent, loving ... children. A part of both of us, binding us together for life."

Life! The necklace was the bait in an entrapment scheme! A diamond ring would be pale in significance compared to the dark centered rose held by the unicorn.

"Stop, Brett," Crystal said, pushing against his shoulders. "Children aren't part of a love affair. Granted I may be a blithe spirit, but being an unmarried mother ..."

Brett's palm covered the slight feminine rounding of her stomach. Smiling, he said presumptuously, "You know about unicorns and flowers; do you know about the birds and the bees? Being lovers makes babies."

"Not in this day and age. Let me assure you, I am not pregnant!"

"Too bad," he muttered, stroking the golden satin of her flesh. "I had hoped to gain total capitulation through pregnancy."

"You're kidding. What would your family think?" Crystal answered her own question. "A *nobody* pregnant by a *Masterson*? Any chance of them accepting me would be annihilated."

"Is that it? The real cause of your reticence? Everything else is a smoke screen?"

Fingering the chain, she neither denied nor confirmed his suspicion. How could she deny the doubts she had had revolving around acceptance by his socially prominent family? Hadn't they selected a bride for him who was socially compatible? Perhaps there was another childhood sweetheart lurking around the homestead. A pang of jealousy stabbed at her heart. Could Brett be manipulated into another loveless arrangement? *History supposedly does repeat itself, doesn't it?* Resolutely she decided to let Brett think his background was the cause of her reticence.

"I'd prefer having the family blessing, but it isn't imperative. You will adjust or they will. I have great faith in your charm. When charm doesn't work, you can steamroller over them!"

He was wrong, Crystal thought, silently unconvinced. She would be the one flattened. It was pointless to discuss family love versus passion.

"We'll see," she replied coolly, unwilling to be persuaded. Don't confuse me with logic, she silently pleaded, I've already made up my mind.

The sound of paws scratching on glass diverted the stream of conversation. Scotty and Mac's patience had been stretched to the limit.

"Bad dogs," Crystal scolded, hurrying to the door. "Shame! You'll mar the glass."

Bounding past their owner, they clamored

into Brett's lap. Their pink tongues flicked over his hands and face.

"Don't let them do that," Crystal instructed, interrupting the joyful reunion.

"I like it," Brett replied, tweaking the long whiskers on Mac's chin, then rubbing behind his ear. "You could take a lesson from your pets," he teased. "I'd arrive with a truckload of cookies if you'd greet me as enthusiastically." Scotty began nudging the pocket of his jacket. "Yeah, boy, I brought you a present."

Widening the opening, the dark head dipped beneath the flap, extracting his favorite treat. Mac immediately nuzzled into the other pocket.

"Don't you dare eat on the furniture. Scat!" Her rapid advance sent Scotty and Mac springing off the sofa and scampering into the kitchen. "You are spoiling my dogs!" she accused.

"What's a few cookie crumbs among friends?" Brett asked, his dark eyes twinkling innocently. Swiping the remainder of his treat off the nubby fabric, he ignored her strangled snort.

Having hastily devoured their cookies, the dogs returned. Crystal couldn't keep her lips clamped together in a grim line when both dogs prettily begged for another treat. Mentally she pictured two humungous terriers too round to sit on their haunches, rolling over as their favorite man displayed empty pockets. She chuckled at the image.

"No more, fellas. Go lie down," Brett instructed, petting each one on the head.

Scotty ambled over to the picture window with Mac sniffing at his nub of a tail.

"Stop that, Mac," Crystal ordered. Brett laughed. "Do you know why dogs sniff at each other?"

"Another biology lesson?" Crystal jested, draping herself on his lap when he beckoned her by slapping his thigh and opening his arms.

"Your education is sadly lacking," he said, snuggling her closer.

"Hmmm," Crystal replied noncommitally. "I have a feeling my horizons are going to be expanded."

Brett grinned, drawing one lock of her long hair between his fingers and wrapping the curl at the end around them. "Once upon a time..."

"A bedtime story?" Crystal broke in, wiggling her bottom.

"Behave!" Playfully he swatted her hip. "Now, where was I? Oh, yes. Once upon a time, before man ruled the world, dogs controlled everything."

"Sort of like the apes in the movie. . . ."

"Hush! You are ruining one of my favorite fables." Crystal put her forefinger over her lips to seal them. "The king and queen decided to have a big party to celebrate the marriage of their beautiful, silky-haired daughter." He stopped long enough to kiss the silk binding his fingers. "It was a party befitting a princess. At the door, each dog checked in its . . . buns."

Her eyebrow raised at the impossible feat. Brett shrugged and grinned.

"It was a courtesy, sort of like gunfighters removing their weapons," he explained, chuckling. "Anyway. A jealous suitor decided to bring an abrupt halt to the celebration. He started a fire. Now, everyone knows fire causes animals to panic. All of the dogs stampeded from the banquet hall. . . . At the door they grabbed any rear end and stuck it on to speed up their departure. And that, young lady, is why today dogs sniff each other."

"They're trying to locate their own rear end?" Crystal said skeptically. "Very clever, Professor Masterson."

"On that happy note I'll bid you adieu," he said, shifting her onto the sofa.

"*Adieu?*" she echoed, flabbergasted. He wasn't going to spend the night? Not resume where they had left off? "I've had my story. Now I'd like to be properly tucked in," she provocatively invited.

Crooking his finger under her chin, he lightly brushed her lips. "Not if you refuse to make an honest man of me." Standing, he straightened the crease in his slacks, then buttoned his suit jacket.

"Next you'll be telling me I won't respect you in the morning."

"I'll admit I'm easy, but I'm not the village punch," he responded, the laughter remaining in his voice. "My self-respect remains intact." Proffering his hand to help her from the couch, he added wryly, "It's my male ego that resembles a target on a military sharp-shooters range."

Fingers lacing through his, Crystal cocked her head upward. "You are the one doing the rejecting." A sense of panic washed over her. Was he going to withdraw completely this time? Another bleak week without him would be agony.

She couldn't conceal the pain furrowing her brow when Brett circumspectly kissed it.

"Why the frown?" he questioned, soothing the wrinkles away with rough fingertips. "Are you going to retreat again?"

"No, love. Simply withholding services."

The double entendre of which specific services wasn't lost on Crystal.

"Starving out the opposition?" she quipped.

Smoldering, hungry eyes slowly descended. "Fasting is good for the soul, but hell on the flesh. Never doubt my wanting you. When I'm alone and close my eyes, I can almost taste your sweetness. In a crowd I subconsciously look for a beautiful brunette with a camera jauntily bouncing on her hip."

"Then stay," she coaxed, sensing his weakening defenses. Watching him closely, she could see the steely control he had exhibited time after time again slipping into place. Damn, she silently cursed. Stalemate!

"If I stay, we'll continue drifting." A hand cupping her cheekbones, he rubbed the tip of his nose against hers, Eskimo-style. "You're off limits."

"Go AWOL," she encouraged huskily, licking her lips in open invitation.

"No, my love. We can't build anything one night at a time." Beside his taunt thigh he snapped his fingers; eyes still locked on her face, he beckoned her pets. "'Night, fellows. Guard her well." Giving Crystal a mock salute and a broad smile, he gave the dogs one last love pat and left.

Closing the door, Crystal vacillated between

congratulating herself for reaffirming her desire for a temporary status and kicking herself for being unable to entice him out of the living room into the bedroom. Smoothing both hands over the satin-tunic top, she wished stronger male hands replaced her own. Turning to the hallway mirror, she stuck her tongue out at the reflection. The childish gesture brought a smile to her face.

The minute black stone winked saucily, drawing her attention to the altered good-luck piece. Fingering the familiar shape of the unicorn soothed her tumultuous emotions. Brett had added to the beauty of the piece of jewelry. Grinning more widely, she admitted to being enchanted by the man as well.

Hugging the thought, she anticipated the challenge Brett had issued. He was positive she desired him more than any other factor, making her refuse his proposal. He had given her a taste of the proverbial apple; could she restrain her appetite for more? A gleeful chuckle slipped from between her love-swollen lips. Mac gave a merry yip in response.

"Boy, he can't win without losing, and I can't lose without winning. Or do I have that backward?"

Chapter Twelve

Jaw dropping, Crystal stared at the intimate back pose of Brett standing in bikini shorts, head turned, winking enticingly. A mild expletive crossed her lips as she slammed the silver copy closed. How had the picture become part of the layout?

Jerking the bottom desk drawer out, she hastily withdrew the packet containing his pictures. Dumping them on the desktop, she frantically searched through them. *Gone!*

Who? Eyes narrowing, she raised her head. *Chad! That miserable, sneaky* ... The name-calling passed the mild expletive stage. A red tide of anger flushed her cheeks. No wonder he had been casting supercilious glances at her all morning. He expected her to blow apart like a bomb at any moment. *Damn it; she wouldn't give him the satisfaction.*

"What did you think of the art department's paste-ups, Chad?" she inquired with saccharin sweetness.

"Not bad." His hand covered a snicker. "The last page was a good clincher."

Casually she picked up a yellow pencil from beside the green ink blotter. Tapping the eraser on the front of the silver sheets, she contemplated strangling Chad. Justifiable homicide, she mused angrily. *Not a court in the land would convict me. I might even get a reward.*

"Competition ought to be stiff when thousands of women read the caption," Clint sneered.

The caption! She had been too distraught by the picture to notice the caption. Shuffling through the pages, she read Chad's handiwork. An audible groan passed from deep in her throat.

"You fool!" she hissed, loosing her cool. "He will sue this fledgling magazine for every penny in its coffers."

"Sue?" Chad gasped. "Didn't you get a release form signed?" A pinched, worried expression replaced the smugness he had displayed earlier.

"Why do you think *I* didn't use any of these pictures?" she inquired, grabbing the stack and waving them at him.

"No woman wants her man being chased by every skirt in St. Louis."

"Is that why you did it? To end everything between Brett and me?" she asked incredulously.

Punching his slipping glasses back to the bridge of his nose, he answered drolly, "I couldn't care less about your love life. I want you off the magazine's staff. It's you or me."

"You fool!" she spat. "I promised him, gave him my word that none of these would be published. When he sees this"—she shoved the silver prints toward his desk—"he'll think I violated that trust." Leaning forward, she asked scornfully, "What do you think? Will he sue?"

"Maybe not." His thick glasses thumped as they struck the top of his desk. "Have you slept with him yet?"

"What?" she sputtered, not believing his audacity. "Are you suggesting..."

"Why not? Women peddle sex for favors all the time."

The fury Crystal had contained was being shaken like a carbonated soda pop. The pencil between her fingers snapped into two pieces.

"Not this woman! You'll take the consequences. Not me!" The jagged edge of the pencil pointed toward Chad.

"Your word against mine," he responded shrewdly.

"Wrong. Brett might not believe in my innocence, but Mike will. He saw the article when we discussed the paper-doll version of the pictures. I'll lose Brett, but by God, you'll lose your job!"

"My job?" he croaked, his face entirely devoid of color. All he needed was two coppers on his eyelids and he could have passed for a corpse. Tears welled in his eyes, then gushed down his face.

Shocked at seeing a grown man cry, Crystal's eyes rounded. Unable to watch, she stood and moved to the file cabinet behind him.

"I can't lose this job," she heard Chad moan between sobs. "It'll be the end of me. I was fired from my last job." A shudder wracked his body. "That's why..." he sniveled, "I sabotaged your work. 'Fraid you'd get my job." Chad held his head in his arms on his desk as he admitted his fears between gulps.

The muscles in Crystal's stomach clenched. The watery confession washed away the major portion of the anger she had felt. How could she kick Chad when he was already down? Pulling two tissues from the box on the cabinet, she tucked them into his hand. In a maternal fashion she patted him on the shoulder.

"Never mind," she soothed. "I'll take the rap." The words passing over her tongue and between her teeth tasted bitter.

Swiveling in his chair, he wrapped his arms tightly around her waist and buried his face against her chest. His thin shoulderblades shivered beneath her touch.

"You're the best. From now on I'll be good to you," he promised like a contrite child.

Reassuringly she stroked his head. "Shhh. I'll take care of the problem with Brett." Trying to get a smile from him, she added, "After all, his is just E.B.S.; you're my partner."

"That tells me exactly where I stand," Crystal heard Brett's drawl coming from behind.

By the time Crystal had untangled herself from the arms tightly holding her and had rushed to the doorway, all she saw was Brett weaving his way between the clerks' desks.

"Brett!" she yelped, rushing out of her office.

Shoulders stiff with military erectness, he strode into the elevator, then turned and punched the down button. The look on his face was one of pure, unadulterated hatred.

Waving her hands, she tried to get him to hold the doors open until she could get there. Eyes forward, she plowed into a paper-piled desk. White sheets flew everywhere. A winter

blizzard could not have been thicker or caused
more damage.

"Sorry," she muttered, charging toward the
closing doors.

Realizing she would never make it, she
veered to the staircase. *I have to stop him,* she
thought wildly. She knew how easily the words
she had spoken could have been misconstrued.
Pushing against the fire door, she burst into the
lobby of the building, huffing and puffing.
Anxiously her amber eyes darted to the elevator. It was empty. Searching for his tall form,
she raced to the front revolving door.

"Gone," she muttered in abject misery.
"Damn, damn, triple damn!"

Shoulders slumped, she headed back into
the building. Didn't Brett know she loved him?
How could he believe she would choose *Chad*
over him? Preposterous! She'd take a mangy
alley cat home before she'd stoop to involving
herself personally with Chad.

She'd give him time to get back to his office, then call him and explain. Once he was
over the shock of finding her in another
man's arms, he would see how ridiculously
funny it was. Wouldn't he?

Upon her return to the fourth floor, a deep
flush of embarrassment climbed up her neck.
Four women were gathered around the desk

she had run into and were busy trying to sort out the mound of papers and restore order. A hush fell over the room as she entered.

No one seemed able to meet her eyes with more than a wary glance. More than a desk overturned had taken place during her brief absence.

"Crystal," Mike's secretary called. "The boss wants to see you ... immediately."

Inwardly Crystal groaned. She wasn't the only one who had previewed the silver sheets. Mike must have seen them too! As scared as the office help were, he must have come out of his office roaring like a lion escaping from the zoo.

The brave words she had spoken to Chad regarding taking the responsibility for the unauthorized picture were ringing in her ears. What was it Mike had told her when he hired her? The gruff words filtered through her mind as she headed toward his office.

"If I tell you a chicken dips snuff, then check under its wing and you'll find a tin box."

Hadn't he told her repeatedly not to get Brett involved in the E.B.S. story? From the incorrect information Mike had, she had not only involved Brett ... he was the final page of the article.

As she glanced over her shoulder as she

pecked on the opaque glass, his secretary gave
her a weak smile, followed by a thumbs-up sig-
nal. With an artificial smile pasted on her face,
Crystal swiftly entered when she heard Mike
roar, "Come in!"

"I see you altered the final version of the
E.B.S. story," Mike commented before she
could even seat herself.

"You don't like it?" Crystal asked, feigning
innocence.

One shaggy gray eyebrow lifted. "No," he
replied succinctly. "Brett won't either."

Unconsciously Crystal flinched. With a false
smile she said glibly, "It is a great shot."

"Fantastic," Mike retorted scathingly. "Care
to tell me how you managed to photograph
Brett so...revealingly? Damn, woman, he's
almost naked!"

Crystal had the grace to flush. The picture
was self-explanatory. Mike was too sharp to
waste a lie on. He knew exactly what had taken
place either before or shortly after the camera
shutter had closed. The memory of their torrid
lovemaking flashed brighter than an electric
strobe across her mind.

"Do you have a release?" he asked impatiently. His fingers strummed in agitation on
the desk.

The question pierced Crystal's momentary

fantasy. "No. But I'll get one," she rashly promised. "I know how expensive changing the picture would be since it has been copper plated." Wringing her hands, she said, "I'll either have the release or I'll..." The words stuck in her craw. "I'll resign."

"Don't worry about resigning," he replied abruptly. "You'll be fired. Brett suing the magazine could have us *all* out of work in a hurry!"

Under normal circumstances Crystal would have laughed at his alarmed state. She didn't. This was far from a laughing matter.

"Damn it, Crystal... You knew Brett had justifiable cause for not wanting any publicity. Why did you do it?"

I didn't do it, her mind shrieked. At one point, in anger, she had considered using his picture... but not *that* one.

"He is a prime example of E.B.S.," she replied, giving the first half truth entering her mind that would remotely resemble a plausible reason.

"Half the population in St. Louis is male, and she chooses *him* as *the* sex symbol," Mike snorted, raising his hands upward to appeal to a higher being. Mike cocked his ear as if awaiting a reply. None forthcoming, he shook his head in disgust. "You have exactly twelve hours to get a release signed, sealed, and delivered to my desk. Might I suggest you take a personal-leave day?''

Company policy required a day's notice to take off for personal business. He was granting immediate leave. Emergency leave was granted on such short notice. Evidently getting the form signed was an emergency!

"Thanks, Mike. I'll go straight to his office. Maybe tonight you should serve crow for the main course and humble pie for dessert,'' she said, grinning ruefully.

"Well, if you don't succeed, I'll exert a little cousinly influence,'' he replied, realizing he had come down hard on her.

Rising to her feet, she accepted the offer with a curt nod. "We'll be there at seven.'' *I hope.*

She debated calling before arriving at the telephone company, but opted for a face-to-face confrontation. The decision was fruitless. Brett had notified his secretary he would be out for the day. Thwarted, Crystal left the telephone building feeling down in the mouth. Was he purposely avoiding her? Impossible, she decided, climbing back in her car and heading toward his condo. It had not been twenty-four hours since he had heard her confess her need, her love, for him. Had he forgotten that quickly?

A few minutes later, as she pulled into the underground parking lot, her spirits lifted when she saw his long silver Cadillac parked in the reserved space for tenants. He must have gone straight home after seeing the imagined wild, passionate embrace, she mused. How uncharacteristic of him. He probably hadn't missed a day of work in years. She knew he was the sort of person who was a faithful, loyal employee.

In the elevator she planned her strategy. First she would explain about being found in Chad's clutches, then, when he had calmed down, she would show him the E.B.S. story. After he signed the form they could spend the afternoon together.

The simple plan was vanquished by the withdrawn, glacial stare bestowed on Crystal when Brett answered the door.

"What do you want?" he asked rudely.

"Jack Frost, I presume?" she quipped, making an effort to melt an iceberg with a radiant smile. "May I come in?"

"I'd rather you didn't," Brett replied, not budging from the doorway.

"That's my line. Shall I forcefully break in while you shout *fire*?" She was beginning to feel conspicuous standing in the hallway, begging entry.

"Your sense of humor and memory are in

fine working order," he complimented wearily. "Unfortunately I'm not up to matching wits. Go back to Chad." Withdrawing into the interior, he began closing the door.

Seeing the door being shut in her face spurred her into action. Taking two steps backward, she catapulted herself against the closing door. A thud later, she was sprawled on the carpet in the entryway, and Brett was swearing profusely as he rubbed a lump on his forehead. The door slammed.

Clambering to her feet, Crystal said with false calmness, "I'm not sorry. You need to have some sense knocked into that thick hard head of yours? I love *you,* damn it... *not Chad*!"

"Sure you do," Brett said, each word dripping with sarcasm. "He is E.B.S.; you are my partner," he quoted in a falsetto voice. Hooking his thumbs in the belt loops of his pants, impatiently he asked, "What do you want from me, woman?"

The bald question took the wind out of her sails. What did she want... *the most*? Right now all she wanted was to get his signature on the form inside the silver prints she had dropped during her ignoble entrance. He obviously wasn't in any frame of mind to listen to her explanation about what he thought he had seen.

"I want your signature," she replied bluntly. "Your picture is in the E.B.S. story. Mike is going to fire me if I don't get it."

His harsh, deep laughter split the air. "You fight dirty, Crystal. You used me to bring Chad to heel; you used my picture in your article; and you used me to allieviate your sexual frustrations." His weight shifted to his other foot uneasily. In a low, menacing voice he asked, "Did you have the release form on the bedstand last night? At the big moment did you plan on shoving it under my nose?"

A ringing slap ended the bitter harangue. The force of the blow jarred Crystal from the tips of her fingers to her shoulderblades.

"You're despicable. You talk about undying love and then accuse me of...prostituting myself for a picture!"

The handprint on his cheek reddened. A vein on his forehead pulsated erratically. "Show me how wrong I am." Picking up the pages on the floor, he flicked through them until he found both the picture and the release form. Scornfully he laughed.

"Great caption, Crystal. 'Playboy of yesteryear, alive, well, and available. Call 555-1111.'

I'll have several weeks of heavy breathing to look forward to when you're gone.'' Again the humorless laugh rent the air.

Snatching the offensive paper from between his fingers, she wadded it into a tight ball and flung it at his chest. Seconds later she was back in the underground parking lot, running to her car.

Miles down the road, vision impaired by the tears cascading down her face, she pulled over to the curb. "I hate you, Brett Masterson! I hate you!'' Fist pounding the steering wheel, she obliterated the deep pain in her chest with the superficial pain in her hand. Deep, heart-wracking sobs drove all thoughts from her mind. Burying her face in her hands, she bawled, heartbroken.

When she had cried until her eyes had run dry, a spasm of hiccups began to torture her chest. She hurt. No one had ever wounded her as deeply. Taking several quick gasps of air, she sought to control her diaphragm without success. Oh, hell, she thought, I'll probably be one of those people who have the hiccups for years and years! Wiping the traces of tears from her face, she started the car and pulled back on the road.

Emotionally exhausted, she ignored the clamor Scotty and Mac made at her unscheduled arrival. Drapes closed, the darkness welcomed by her irritated eyes, she mechanically trod into the bedroom and flopped on the bed. Legs pulled up to her chest, arms wrapped tightly around them, she racked her brain for a logical explanation for the brutal verbal abuse.

Had she subconsciously been using Brett?

"No. No. No," she fervently denied out loud.

She could't deny her original intention of using his picture, but when she had uncovered the scandal he had suffered through, hadn't she dispelled any thought of the original plan? She had. The article had been submitted *without* his picture.

Brett's claiming she had used him to bring Chad to heel was the most ludicrous idea she had ever heard. She should have told Brett all along of the running feud they had. Why hadn't she? Because you didn't want him to know working for *SLM* wasn't all peaches and cream, she answered honestly.

Had she used him to satisfy her sexual hunger? If she had, he only had himself to blame. He was the one responsible for the insatiable craving. Had they never touched, never kissed, she would have been perfectly happy devoting herself to her job.

"Liar," she muttered. "You fell in love with

him when you took your first picture in the park. You haven't devoted yourself to your career since then.''

Groaning at the realization, she stretched out on her back and stared blindly at the ceiling. "It's all Chad's fault," she said thickly, placing the blame where it belonged. "He's getting off scot-free while I'm forced to wallow in his mess!"

The phone ringing on the bedside table made her sit bolt upright. "Hello," Crystal said, picking it up on the first ring; hoping it was Brett.

"Good work, Crystal! Brett sent the signed form over by, er, special messenger.''

"He what?"

"You heard me. Whew! That takes a load off my mind. He left a note for you; shall I read it?"

"Please."

"See you at Mike's at seven," Mike read. "I guess he won't be picking you up, kiddo. You'll have to use the shoe-leather express."'

"Right," she numbly replied, trying to coagulate the change of events.

"Jane thought your story was hilarious."

"How did she see it?"

"Well...er, she stopped in at the office and read it while she was waiting for the ambulance."

"Ambulance! Are you sick?" she asked, remembering how worried and ill he had appeared earlier.

"No. I'm fine. Listen, kiddo, I don't have time to yammer. *Someone* on this staff has to work!"

Crystal heard his other line buzz.

"Got to go. See you tonight."

The line was disconnected before she could offer to come back in for the rest of the day. She knew she should be bouncing up and down happily, but somehow saving her job didn't penetrate the heavy cloud of depression enveloping her.

Why had Brett signed the release? The likelihood of his changing his mind was remote. Did he plan on enjoying his notoriety? Or could it possibly be this was his way of apologizing for completely losing control of his temper?

Brett *had* lost control. Calm conservative, walk-away-from-unpleasantness Brett had lost his cool. Blown apart at the seams! Never again did she want to witness, much less bear the brunt of, his temper.

The remainder of the afternoon was spent mulling over what had, and had not, taken place in their relationship. One thought dominated all others... *I love him.* The time for war skirmishes and games had ended. Not one of her reasons for procrastinating or restraining their relationship held water. They had, each and every one of them, been excuses hiding the truth.

Admitting she cared more about Brett than she did her job stripped away the final pretense. Underneath the womanly curves and feminine cosmetics she was the same insecure, unconfident teenager with braces and skin blemishes who had not been invited to the prom.

She had been afraid to love a man...any man. By hiding under the facade of being a woman totally dedicated to her career, she had eliminated, emasculated, most men. But not Brett. He had broken through her defenses. Skillfully he had captured her love and her heart. Even the hard pebble core was mush.

For the first time as an adult woman she was vulnerable. Tonight Brett would hold a very fragile heart in his hands. He could callously toss it aside or cherish it as a prize possession. Crystal did not know which he would choose.

"I'm not afraid of love," she whispered, putting the thought into concrete, spoken words. "I'm not afraid."

Warm summer breezes swirled her blue halter-top sun dress around her legs as Crystal circled the tennis court for the second time.

"Coward!" she chastized under her breath.

No amount of conjecturing, or reasoning, or positive thinking could keep the goosebumps from prickling her skin. She felt as though she were in the middle of a championship tennis match with a bowling ball, and it was her turn to serve.

Delaying her arrival would make matters worse. Resolutely she changed direction, and with a steady, purposeful step, marched to her impending doom.

"Come in, Crystal," Jane welcomed warmly, ushering her back to the patio. "White wine okay?"

The smell of hickory smoke wafted into the apartment when she slid the glass door open. Mike and Brett courteously arose when they saw her.

Honey-colored eyes flowed toward eyes blacker than midnight. Silently they each assessed the temperament of the other. Can he see how much I love him? Crystal wondered. Does he know, above all else, I need his love? A smile crinkled laugh lines at the corners of the dark eyes in telepathic response.

His arms spread wide, palms upward. Not hesitating, she stepped into them and wrapped her own around his waist. Burrowing her face against his chest, she inhaled his familiar fragrance and listened to the increased thudding of his heart.

Flushing prettily, Crystal eased away, but not before Brett dropped a loving kiss on her forehead. His arm slipped possessively around her waist, and they stood side by side.

Beaming, Mike motioned for them to be seated. "Well, now," he said, rubbing his hands together, "as soon as *my* bride appears we'll celebrate the completion of a job well done."

Crystal suspected Mike was referring to more than the publication of the E.B.S. story. Cocking her head in his direction, shooting a questioning glance, she knew she was right when he chuckled. The wrought-iron chair nudging the back of her knees made them buckle. A boyish grin was on Brett's face too.

Jane slipped through the patio door with a tray of crystal stemware and a bottle of wine. Placing the tray on the table, she grinned mischievously at Crystal and winked.

"Who's the gift for, darling?" Mike inquired, reaching for the foil-capped wine bottle.

Crystal automaticaly accepted the flat, thin package when Jane handed it to her, saying, "Now that this month's magazine is put to bed, I thought I'd reward you with something special."

"Very sweet of you, my dear," Mike said, smiling warmly at his spouse. "Shall we propose a toast before or after the gift giving?"

"I'd like to make the toast, if I may?" Crystal said impetuously.

All eyes were on her. *Now,* her heart commanded. Raising an empty champagne glass toward Mike, she gathered her wits while she watched the effervescent wine being poured.

As she touched the rim of Mike's glass, a bell-like tone broke the silence. "To Mike... may his tennis game continue to improve... and keep four paces behind mine."

"Hear! Hear!" Mike enthused with a chuckle, clicking their glasses together.

"To Jane"—their glasses touched—"a bride after thirty years of marriage."

"Hear! Hear," Jane echoed, squeezing her husband's thigh.

Crystal turned to the dark, handsome man beside her and touched the edge of his glass. Courageously she murmured the words Brett had waited to hear.

"To Brett... my love... my life...." She watched his expression closely as she broke the bonds shackling them to a temporary love affair. "Will you marry the girl you have changed into a complete woman? Will you marry *me*?"

Setting his wine down, he cupped her hand,

which contained the wineglass. Eyes never leaving hers, Brett brought the pale amber liquid to his lips and drained the glass.

The intimate acceptance made Crystal feel as though the tiny bubbles had entered her own bloodstream and were heatedly coursing toward her heart. It was the height of romantic gestures, made doubly exhilarating by his willingness to show his love in front of others. Shouting it from the rooftop, pasting it on a billboard, sky-writing his love, could not have been more explicit.

An enthusiastic hug from Jane brought her back to reality. Mike was pumping Brett's hand up and down like a rusty water pump while clapping him soundly on the back.

Dinner was a gay occasion. Teasingly Mike made suggestions on how to handle a woman, while Jane demonstrated, humorously, how she was the one doing the managing. Crystal laughed so hard at times her sides hurt.

Neither Brett nor Crystal could have told anyone what they had eaten, or why even the silliest of statements was indescribably hilarious. They were on a strict diet of happiness. Each time their hands, legs, or eyes met, the inner joy they felt generated a warm glow around them.

As soon as etiquette would allow, Brett proposed one last toast to his future bride and suggested they leave to make wedding plans.

Handing Crystal the unopened package, which had fallen to the ground during the excitement and been forgotten, Jane kissed her lightly on the cheek and shoved both of them out the front door.

Chapter Thirteen

"When?" Brett asked, tugging her down the path.

She didn't need to ask what he was talking about. She knew. "A six-month engagement is standard," she replied, an impish light twinkling in her honey-colored eyes, brighter than the stars overhead.

"Too old-fashioned. How about a modern three days?" he riposted.

"Three days! We won't have time to notify your family or mine in that length of time."

"A week, then...no more."

"But, Brett, I have to find a wedding dress, send out invitations, order flowers, rustle up some bridesmaids...there are a million and one things that cannot be done in a week."

"Three days!" Hauling her into his arms he

kissed her with a hunger that denied a waiting period of even twenty-four hours. He devoured her lips as though he were starving.

Instantaneously passion flared. Crystal responded with a ferocious need of her own. Only his lips could quench her thirst, which was as powerful as his hunger. Their tongues darted back and forth, capturing the dark recesses of each other's mouth.

A shudder made him physically tremble against her as he said hoarsely, "Dont make me wait. Marry me as soon as possible. I'll be stark raving crazy if you don't."

Peppering his neck with kisses, she whispered, "Come home with me. Love me now."

Pressing his hands over her rounded derriere, he groaned deeply. "Three days. Say it! *Three days.*"

"Three days!" she shouted, loud enough for all of the neighbors to hear.

Lifting her bodily off the ground, swinging her round and round, Brett gave a loud whoop of exuberant delight and tossed his head back, laughing joyously.

"Total capitulation?"

"Unconditional surrender!" she affirmed. "Now, take me home and pillage what you have conquered."

"Never pillage," he growled as he sensually let her slide down the length of his muscular torso. "Worship, cherish, protect, but never pillage."

Minutes later Scotty and Mac were outside the bedroom door munching on the cookies Brett had hidden in his suit jacket, while their mistress and new master were locked away in the privacy of her room.

Brett's eyes undressed Crystal before she had undone the first button or lowered the zipper in the back of her dress. "You're a divinely unusual woman, Crystal Clare Lake."

Provocatively she raised her arms to untie the knot at the back of her neck. With a sharp tug, the blue cotton bodice dropped to her waist. Fastening on the smooth, rounded globes, his eyelids lowered fractionally as she ran her hands up from the waist, then cupped their swelling heaviness.

She knew when she saw him moisten his lips that he was intent on restraining himself. Swaying her hips in an exaggerated fashion, she advanced toward him.

"Unusual enough to break through your self-control again?"

"Self-control in lovemaking guarantees satisfaction," Brett responded, his eyes shifting from her pendulous breasts to her slender hips.

"You blew your cool when you thought I was in love with Chad. Do you *want* me enough...?"

The scant inches between them abruptly closed when Brett pulled her into his arms and fervently stopped the question with his lips, teeth, and tongue. Strong hands burrowed beneath the waistband of her dress and lingerie, digging into her flesh as he rotated their hips together.

"I'd like to rip off your clothes, fling you on the bed, and plunge into your womanly softness. It's been a lifetime since we've made love."

As he stiffened his wrists, fabric momentarily sliced into her waist before the pressure broke the fastening and the zipper. Unhampered by the bindings on the dress, he stretched her flimsy underwear and thrust it downward in one smooth motion.

Stepping from the pool of clothing at her feet, Crystal caught Brett off-balance as he was rising and pitched him backward onto the bed. Her nakedness rubbed against the silkiness of his shirt and the coarser fabric of his trousers.

"Love me, Brett," she encouraged, unbuckling his belt and making short work of removing his trousers.

Brett shifted her from the dominant position

while caressing her from shoulder to waist. "Your skin is afire; hotter than a raging fever," he whispered hoarsely, excited by the fingernails raking, scoring through the shirt on his back.

"Now, Brett. Don't wait."

Hooking her leg around his upper thigh, she wedged herself beneath him. She pressed against him, luring him closer. Brett groaned, unable to resist. Raising her writhing hips, he drove into the welcoming heat with one swift, powerful thrust.

"Again," Crystal mumbled, delight evident in the tone of her voice. She wanted him . . . all of him . . . buried in the core of her femininity.

"I'm home. Where I belong," he whispered, leaning forward, nuzzling the sweetness of her breasts with his lips.

Crystal intuitively knew he was deliberately slowing the pace, striving to bridle his runaway passion. Clasping her hands at the back of his neck, she lightly applied pressure, which encouraged him to gorge rather than taste the fullness of her breasts.

The final thread snapped. Deep rhythmical groans could be heard as he thrust with his hips, massaged with his hands, and suckled avariciously at her breasts. Joy spread with lightning force throughout her. Brett was uninhibitedly ravishing her, and she loved it.

Previously his main concern had been for her gratification, not his. He had physically treated her as though she were a fragile piece of china. A treasure to be admired, gently stroked, satisfied, but never to be the recipient of unbridled passion.

When he shouted her name from the passionate peaks they had jointly climbed, Crystal's heart felt as though it would burst with love. She was neither the conqueror nor the conquered. At last they were equals.

As he collapsed heavily, the buttons on his shirt pressed into her sensitive skin. Softly she whimpered in discomfort.

Brett rolled to his side. "Crystal? Oh, love, have I hurt you?"

"Your buttons," she gasped between short pants.

"Buttons?" Glancing down, he seemed amazed when he saw the wrinkled, damp shirt. Using one hand, he unbuttoned the shirt, removed it, and tossed it toward a nearby chair. A smile lifted his lips upward, as though a pleasant thought had passed through his mind.

"Why the grin?" Crystal asked, ruffling her fingers over the exposed mat of hair on his chest.

"You'll call off the wedding if I tell you," he replied with a devilish grin.

Cyrstal playfully tweaked his flat nipple.

"Ouch," Brett yelped, swatting her hand away.

"Why the Mona Lisa?" she quizzed. "I promise not to renege on the wedding date."

"I've never made love with my clothes on," he confided. "It was...fantastic."

Crystal matched his grin. Taking his hand, she raised it to her lips, kissed each tip, folded it over her smaller hand, and nibbled on each knuckle.

Brett inhaled sharply, withdrawing his hand. Through slit eyes she saw him grimace as his fingers disappeared beneath the pillow. When she grabbed his wrist, Brett resisted her effort to extract it. Not one to be outwitted by brute strength, she lifted the pillow and tossed it aside. Her mouth rounded into a small *O* when she saw four of his knuckles were badly grazed.

"How did you do this?" she questioned in dismay.

Brett looked at his fist and grinned boyishly. "I administered a small dose of poetic justice."

"With your knuckles?"

"Justice was swift in this case."

"Brett!"

"Crystal!" he mimicked, kissing her on the forehead. "Weren't you even mildly curious as to why I signed the release form?"

Mutely she nodded her head up and down.

"Chad and I had a little...uh, talk. After some persuasion," Brett flexed his hand into a fist, "he wisely decided to admit the truth."

"You beat him up?" Crystal was torn between applauding his actions and reprimanding him for interfering in her business. She grinned, silently clapping her hands. "Did he bleed a lot, I hope?"

"Bloodthirsty wench," he said, laughing. "Want the gory details?"

Again she bobbed her head, anxious for him to fill in the missing pieces as to what had happened that afternoon.

"He didn't bleed at all the first time I whacked him." Crystal couldn't mask the disappointment she felt. "But he has a lovely black eye." A note of triumph had entered his voice.

"You hit him more than once? Knowing Chad, one blow should have had him on hands and knees crawling toward the door."

"I picked him up by the scruff of the neck and gave him a nose alteration."

"You're kidding," Crystal said, stifling a giggle with her fingertips.

"Then he began babbling like a brook. It's also when one of the secretaries entered and let out a milk-curdling yell at the top of her lungs.

A few minutes later the ambulance arrived and carted off his carcass."

Blinking, Crystal juggled the pieces of the puzzle together. "You were the 'special messenger' Mike said brought the release form?"

This time Brett was the one doing the nodding. "Speaking of Mike...what was the gift Jane gave you?"

"I don't know. I didn't unwrap...the package." A wink filled the pause. Spying the foil gift wrap beside their hastily shed clothing, she retrieved it and returned to the bed.

"I'll share." Tearing off the envelope, she tossed it to Brett. "You read the note; I'll open the gift."

Hauling himself up against the headboard, he flipped the envelope open and removed the card. "'You earned this,'" he read out loud.

"That's all?" she questioned, ripping the wrapping off the package.

Doubling over in a gale of laughter, Crystal laid the contents of the package on the bed for Brett to see. It was a glossy, black-and-white picture of a man whose fingertips, in peek-a-boo fashion, had lowered his boxer shorts, revealing a rear end embossed with a tattooed heart. Below the heart were two words: JANE FOREVER.

Brett took one look and burst into boisterous

guffaws. Clinging to each other, they rolled with laughter.

"Too bad I can't get Mike to sign a release form!" Tears streaming down her face, Crystal asked, "Would you do that for me?"

"I'm no copycat," Brett said, as though affronted by the suggestion. Hugging, tickling, laughing, he added, "Mine will be a unicorn with a rose!"

Harlequin Photo ~ *Calendar* ~

Turn Your Favorite Photo into a Calendar.

JULY 1984

The Browns

Uniquely yours, this 10 x 17½″ calendar features your favorite photograph, with any name you wish in attractive lettering at the bottom. A delightfully personal and practical idea!

Send us your favorite color print, black-and-white print, negative, or slide, any size (we'll return it), along with **3** proofs of purchase (coupon below) from a June or July release of Harlequin Romance, Harlequin Presents, Harlequin Superromance, Harlequin American Romance or Harlequin Temptation, plus $5.75 (includes shipping and handling).

- -

Get this book FREE!

Mail to:

Harlequin Reader Service

In the U.S.	In Canada
2504 West Southern Ave.	P.O. Box 2800, Postal Station A
Tempe, AZ 85282	5170 Yonge St., Willowdale, Ont. M2N 5T5

YES! I want to be one of the first to discover **Harlequin American Romance.** Send me FREE and without obligation *Twice in a Lifetime.* If you do not hear from me after I have examined my FREE book, please send me the 4 new **Harlequin American Romances** each month as soon as they come off the presses. I understand that I will be billed only $2.25 for each book (total $9.00). There are no shipping or handling charges. There is no minimum number of books that I have to purchase. In fact, I may cancel this arrangement at any time. *Twice in a Lifetime* is mine to keep as a FREE gift, even if I do not buy any additional books.

154-BPA-NAXC

Name _____ (please print)

Address _____ Apt. no. _____

City _____ State/Prov. _____ Zip/Postal Code _____

Signature (If under 18, parent or guardian must sign.)

AMR-SUB-2